MARY JANE BEAUFRAND

DARK RIVER

LITTLE, BROWN AND COMPANY

NEW YORK   BOSTON

Little, Brown and Company

Hachette Book Group
237 Park Avenue, New York, NY 10017
Visit our website at www.lb-teens.com

Little, Brown and Company is a division of Hachette Book Group, Inc.
The Little, Brown name and logo are trademarks of Hachette Book Group, Inc.

The publisher is not responsible for websites (or their content) that are not owned by the publisher.

First Paperback Edition: April 2012
First published in hardcover as *The River* in February 2010 by Little, Brown and Company

The Edgar® name is a trademark of the Mystery Writers of America.

Library of Congress Cataloging-in-Publication Data

Beaufrand, Mary Jane.
  [River]
  Dark river / by Mary Jane Beaufrand.—1st pbk. ed.
    p. cm.
  Summary: Teenager Ronnie's life is transformed by the murder of a ten-year-old neighbor for whom she babysat, and who had helped Ronnie adjust to living at a country inn on the banks of the Santiam River in Hoodoo, Oregon.
  ISBN 978-0-316-19905-6
  [1. Murder—Fiction. 2. Taverns (Inns)—Fiction. 3. Running—Fiction. 4. Rivers—Fiction. 5. Moving, Household—Fiction. 6. Oregon—Fiction.] I. Title.
  PZ7.B3805782Riv 2012
  [Fic]—dc23   2011025417

10 9 8 7 6 5 4 3 2 1

RRD-C

Printed in the United States of America

para Juancho

1

I suppose there are worse things than being soggy and dateless and shoveling bunny carcasses into a garbage bin on Valentine's Day, but if there are, I can't think of any. Dad might say being dead in a ditch is worse. Mom would say being dead in a ditch wearing tattered underwear is worse still, at which point Dad might say dead is dead, what does underwear have to do with it anyway, and Mom would shut him up with a pumpkin bar delicately spiced with nutmeg and cinnamon, slathered with cream cheese frosting, which Dad would eat thinking he had cleverly won his case, while the real winner went back to the kitchen to check on her rack of lamb.

Be that as it may, it was ten at night on Valentine's Day, the most romantic day of the year. Fred the Eagle had dropped his latest kill on the back porch again and some of our guests had complained, so I went out to deal with the problem before the neighborhood dogs did. This being February and the western side of the Cascade Mountains, I hadn't been outside for a minute before I was marinated in cold rainwater. I did my best to deal with the carcass problem quickly, while inside the inn diners wearing shades of red and pink had graduated from tables in the café to the sofas around the river rock fireplace in the sunken living room, where they snuggled, forking chocolate fondue into each other's mouths, flush with heat and growing passion. I had never felt so *outside*, as though I weren't a real girl made of flesh and blood but some spirit made of rainwater, doomed forever to hover around windows of places I couldn't enter.

"I've been dumped," said a voice behind me, drawing me back to my own skin. I turned around to see a dark figure in a rain parka and thick-soled boots stomp up the porch steps. He pulled back his hood and I exhaled. It was Ranger Dave.

"What do you mean, dumped?" I said. I was still thinking of an eagle pecking at a bunny and then *dumping* it on our back lawn.

"Dumped. D-U-M-P-E-D. Like a bald tire or a three-legged dog," he said. It was a weird comparison but I understood. Our place was the last building on a dead-end road in the middle of nowhere. Random people decided that this stretch was great for getting rid of things they no longer needed. Tires, puppies, kittens, Styrofoam coolers — it all turned up in our ditches. Including, apparently, Ranger Dave.

Poor guy. His face seemed to have eroded, like an embankment worn away by a swift current. He needed help fast. I'd have to postpone feeling sorry for myself. I hoisted the bunny carcass into the bin marked YARD WASTE and stowed the shovel against the house.

"Let's get you inside," I said.

As Ranger Dave shook the water off his parka in the sun porch, I leaned on the carved-beaver banister at the top of the stairs that led down to the Astro Lounge. "Dad!" I yelled. "Ranger Dave's here!"

Dad's head appeared at the bottom of the stairs. He was drying a huge beer stein. We'd been country innkeepers for almost a year, but I still hadn't gotten used to the change in my father. He had morphed from Republican Attorney Dad to Hairy Viking Dad. He had facial hair. He wore flannel.

"Veronica, what have I said about shouting?" he yelled just as loudly as I had. He took in all the rainwater sluicing off me and onto the carpet. "Get a towel and change your shirt, please. And wash your hands!"

I ignored him. "Ranger Dave is having a crisis."

Dad and I stared at each other for a beat. I continued to drip.

"What kind of crisis?"

"Girl kind."

Dad kept wiping, even though the stein was clean and dry. "Be right there," he finally said.

Ranger Dave, meanwhile, either didn't hear me broad-casting his woe, or didn't care. He took off his boots and shuffled over to the hearth, where he carefully swept little embers back into the fireplace. As an employee of the U.S. Forest Service, he was always on the lookout for anything untended and emitting smoke.

When Dad emerged he was holding two bottles of Black Butte Porter, one of which he handed to Ranger Dave.

"What is it, dude? What's going on?" Dad asked. I don't think my father had ever had a cool friend before, so now he got all embarrassing when Ranger Dave was around. He called him *man* and *dude* and even slouched. Ranger Dave was in his thirties and had that long, grunge-band hair, so it was okay for him to at least pretend to be hip; but on Dad it just seemed wrong. He should stick to his new strengths. Chopping trees. Eating manly breakfasts. Sacking villages.

"Kristi dumped me," Ranger Dave said, not looking at my father as he said it — not looking at any of us.

"Oh," Dad said, trying to look serious, stroking his beard

4

to hide his smirk. Kristi's boobs were bigger than her IQ. She didn't deserve him. And dumping him on Valentine's Day? That was cold. Colder than runoff.

Ranger Dave sighed. "And I thought she might have been the one."

"Seriously?" I interrupted. "I mean, she listened to Christian rock. Don't you hate Christian rock? I thought you said it was an oxymoron."

"I thought it was cute," he said, whacking a burning log.

"That is not cute, it's pathetic," Dad said, rolling his eyes. "Even I know that."

"And remember what you used to say about Kristi's hair?" I prodded.

Dad winked at me and mouthed the words *good one* behind Ranger Dave's back.

"I said she could punch a hole in the ozone layer above her vanity table with all the Aqua Net," Ranger Dave admitted.

Dad smiled. The two of us, working together, had forced a confession. Ranger Dave's case for heartbreak had just collapsed into a heap of black embers. Now we could all get on with our lives.

But rather than feeling better, Ranger Dave seemed worse. He put the poker down and didn't even touch his beer, just slouched against the fireplace and sighed as though all the air had been beaten out of him. And Dad? He took our inability to cheer up our guest as his own personal failure. He sat there, stroking his beard, extracting little flakes of dead skin, which he rolled into little pill shapes and flicked onto the carpet.

"Come on, man," Dad said gently, urging him downstairs. "I'll let you kick my butt at darts."

"That's okay, Paul. I don't really feel like playing right now."

Now Dad was really alarmed. Ranger Dave was always up for a game.

Fortunately, at this point, the kitchen door swung open and Mom came out. Her brown hair was secured with a banana clip on the back of her head, and her white chef's smock and black-checked pants were baggy over her thin frame, making her look like a hip-hop cook.

She carried a tray covered with an elaborate linen napkin. She placed it on Ranger Dave's lap. Suddenly we were surrounded. Our dinner guests stopped smooching; our wait staff, including Daisy and Wanda, not to mention Tomás and Gretchen, my only friends in town, pushed forward with the promise of witnessing something spectacular.

What would Mom offer him? Cardamom bread? Northwest pizza with smoked salmon, roasted red peppers, and feta cheese? Sacher torte, so dense and rich, each bite landed like semisweet buckshot in your stomach?

With a flourish, she whisked the napkin away, revealing a

bag of marshmallows, two slabs of Hershey's chocolate, and a box of graham crackers. She speared a marshmallow on a fondue fork for Ranger Dave and held it out to him, as if he were a child of five. "Here ya go," she said.

I held my breath. Mom could usually read people's hunger with an uncanny level with accuracy, but she was wrong on this one. Ranger Dave, when he wasn't live-trapping aggressive bears or putting out brush fires, was Mr. Ultra Healthy Marathon Man. He once told me he survived a whole week on nothing but bottled water, bananas, and orange GU gel. To him, food was fuel.

S'mores? Mom might as well have offered him a big plate of Styrofoam.

I held my breath as Ranger Dave took the fondue fork and stuck the marshmallow by the embers of the fire. He was humoring Mom. Had to be. We all watched as his marshmallow turned from white to golden to brown and finally black. He pulled it out of the hearth, blew the flame out, and put the hot, black goo in the chocolate graham sandwich Mom held out for him.

He devoured his s'more, then licked the gunk off his fingers one by one. When he was done he carefully closed his eyes. "Disgusting," he pronounced.

But he reached for another.

Around us, people politely applauded and Mom circulated the s'mores plate around the rest of them. You could tell what they were thinking: *I always liked s'mores, but now it's okay to admit it because Claire Severance serves them.* Dad, meanwhile, poured more champagne to anyone who wanted it, all the while smiling at the shadow Mom cast over the soft firelight, a shadow that seemed to cover all of us like a blanket. She'd worked her magic yet again. Dad knew she would; Ranger Dave knew she would (which is why he'd come to us to begin with); our guests and employees had known as well. Mom's culinary powers were legendary. There was nothing she couldn't put right with food.

Nothing, that is, except for me.

Don't get me wrong: I had some decent days — days when I didn't dwell too much on what I'd lost when we moved here, like coffee shops, Nordstrom, clubs with all-ages shows, a school with funding for arts programs.

But then there were other nights when I couldn't filter out the loneliness, and I would lie awake torturing myself, listening to the sounds of the Santiam River running through the backyard, pretending it was just the familiar city cries of the drunks and the meth addicts staggering home from an after-hours show at the Crystal Ballroom.

There was nothing wrong with my life that going home — my real home — couldn't correct.

At least that was what I thought that Valentine's Day, when I still hoped I could be fixed — when I hoped all of us could be fixed. Now I know better. I know there are things

we can understand and control, and then there is the wilderness of the unknowable. Our inn was situated on the frontier
between the two — the last building on a dead-end road;
beyond us there were only trees and mountains and sky and
river — always the river.

And what happened there, at the boundary between the
wild and the tame? That I need more strength to tell. Best to
stop here with marshmallows and chocolate.

2

Lost lost lost . . .

The next morning was Saturday. When I woke up the river had a new mood. I thought I'd heard every noise it could make. When the water was high and swift and muddy, it seemed to be shouting; when it was low and treacherous and soothing, it was almost like a lullaby, one of the lovely but really brutal ones. *Come, dip your toes in my glacial goodness. I will rock you to sleep, and then dash your head against a submerged boulder.*

I'd heard the river angry, I'd heard the river playful, but until that morning I'd never heard the river grieve.

My bedroom was in the attic under a sloping ceiling — a scrawny room that must once have belonged to the hired help or a very cold nun when my great-grandmother first ran Patchworks during the Depression. Back then it was a kind of homey barracks for lumberjacks — a place where a woman with a genteel southern lilt served stacks of biscuits and sweet corn on the cob to men who wanted to remember they weren't one hundred percent wild.

The crow's nest (as Mom called my room) was in the corner on the river side and had a turret with a territorial view. And man, did it cover a lot of territory — rushing water, tall trees, rolling foothills — if I opened the window in winter and leaned out I could almost see the Hoodoo Ski Bowl. But since I didn't ski it was no big deal. I felt no need to conquer mountains or speed down them. Since I was a runner, my attitude was: downhill is cheating.

My room was also the noisiest in the place, especially in a storm. Between the rain slapping the roof and the white water rushing out back, most of the time I woke up feeling pelted. But not that morning. That morning I felt more adrift than usual, as though someone had cut an anchor.

I got out of bed and smoothed the three layers of antique quilts behind me. As I did, I closed my eyes and listened. It definitely seemed as though the river were crying.

I looked out the window. The water was brown and high, but we seemed in no danger of flooding, so I shook off the creepy feeling as I pulled on my sweats and dashed downstairs.

Dad was sitting at his favorite table in front of the picture windows in the café, eating his three-berry bran waffles and looking up every so often to make sure Fred the Eagle was still in his aerie in the treetops along the opposite bank.

I was hoping to sneak past him but he looked up and saw me.

"Hold on, missy. Where do you think you're going?"

Just once I would have liked to have gotten away without him harassing me. My Saturday morning run was my one hour of freedom a week. And to think: months ago I imagined that when he went on serotonin inhibitors I'd be able to get away with more stuff. All the drugs had done was make him more vigilant.

"To Tiny's and back." That was my loop. About a 10K. It took me along the Santiam River Road, past the Kid for Sale sign, past the Santiam National Forest Ranger Station, to Tiny's Garage, which was next to Highway 22, then reverse.

"Got your cell?"

I pulled it out of my sweatshirt pocket and showed it to him.

"Is it juiced?"

I nodded.

He looked at his watch and clicked a button. "I'll call Tiny," he said.

Dad said he got the chills just thinking of me galli-vanting along that isolated road (his word — *gallivant*), so he alerted our neighbors to keep an eye out for me: the Armstrongs at the Kid for Sale sign; Ranger Dave (hope-fully less brokenhearted this morning); and finally, Tiny of Tiny's Garage and Minit-Mart. I suppose the neighbor-hood watch was sweet, but they weighed me down. Without neighbors I could've shaved thirty seconds off my best time, easy.

Mom poked her head out of the kitchen. Ropes of raw dough were peeling off her arms like extra layers of skin. "There's a breakfast burrito for you on the warmer," she said, and went back to slapping a loaf into shape.

I had no desire to eat. Dad had already set his watch; it was time to go.

I burst through the wooden door and into the chilly damp air. It was raining biblically hard, but that made it perfect running weather. I took my first step across the porch and nearly tripped over a two-by-four plank with three mud pies arranged neatly on top, each with a sprig of a fat purple blos-som (lupine?) sticking up like a birthday candle. *Whoa, great presentation*, I thought. *Mom would be impressed.*

I knew who left us the present. Karen, third of four Armstrong children, she of the blue whale rain slicker and cross-shaped scar on her forehead, Kid for Sale. I babysat for her and her brothers and sister yesterday while their parents

13

grabbed a bite at the inn. These mud pies must be Karen's way of saying thank you.

I nudged them to the side of the door and began what would be a very long race.

∞

Of all the buildings in Hoodoo, ours was the only one with "curb appeal." Everyone else focused their gardening skills on their backyards since that was where the river was. Their front yards were either a quarter mile of grit, or a quarter mile of grit peppered with rusted pickups and unfenced, unleashed mongrels. At first I was afraid of these canines, some of whom were large and imposing, running free, but I soon learned that most dogs think of runners as a pack. Sometimes by the time I reached Tiny's I was running with a posse of six dogs. Today, before I ran up to the Armstrongs' house, I'd only picked up Trixie, an energetic terrier, and Thor, a giant, lean German shepherd with a huge bark and a half-masted ear, which made him look always perplexed. Thor was harmless except for the parasites crawling on his belly and ears.

This morning Thor — with his crooked but functional sonar — heard the cries before I did.

"Karen! Karen!"

I rounded the bend and there was Mr. Armstrong standing by his mailbox where the Kid for Sale sign used to be.

He was a compact guy with sandy brown hair and leathery skin of someone who worked outside a lot — which he did, being in construction. Behind him, his yard was being chewed to mud by three stubborn goats.

Mr. Armstrong was worried about something. He tried to hide it, but anxiety was dusting his face like pollen.

"Morning." I nodded.

"Have you seen Karen?" he asked.

"No," I said. And in my heart I felt something do a light somersault. I should've been used to it by now. Karen was an explorer — always charting new places and experiences. When she was off trailblazing she didn't always remember to check in. But she always came back.

I remembered my foot connecting with the mud pies before I started out. "I think she was at the inn earlier. She left us a present. But I haven't seen her."

Mr. Armstrong smiled, but he was holding his breath. "I hope she isn't down by the river. She knows she's not supposed to go there alone."

At that moment, even though I was saturated, I got a chill. On days like these with the snowcaps beginning to melt, the rapids were swift. *Lost lost lost* . . . even here I could hear the river wailing. *Nothing's wrong*, I told myself. *She disappears all the time.*

"I'm sure she's fine. I'll bring her home if I see her." I glanced at my watch. "I should be back in thirty-four minutes.

15

If we haven't found her by then, I'll help you beat the brush."

Mr. Armstrong sighed and looked at his own watch. "Thirty-three. You've got time to make up."

"For Karen? I'll make it in thirty-two."

I smiled at him in what I hoped was a confident, reassuring way. Then I waved and left, happy to be gone. Mr. Armstrong's worry was so palpable it felt like a wall. Some things, I was discovering, you can't run past.

⌒

By the time my pack and I hit the Santiam National Forest Ranger Station, Thor and Trixie and I had picked up Bailey, a mutt that looked like a normal golden retriever from the chest up, but his legs were short and stubby, like a basset's. It was hard to take Bailey seriously. Those stubby legs made him look like a real clown.

The sign in front of the ranger station announced that the danger of a forest fire was low today. I spat the rainwater that had funneled from my hair, down my nose, and into my mouth. I once made the mistake of suggesting to Ranger Dave that his pie chart should have a "Well, duh," setting for days like this. And he'd rounded on me, furious, poking a lean finger at my chest. "Do you know how much acreage we lost last summer? Have you even *seen* the east side of the pass? That burn was so out of control we're lucky no one got killed."

At the time I apologized sincerely and offered him more Penn Cove Mussels with ancho chile salsa, but I think that was the moment I realized that Hoodoo was so different from my old life I could take nothing for granted. In Hoodoo, I couldn't even make jokes about the weather.

∞

This morning Ranger Dave was sitting on the covered porch, dry and smug, sipping a mug of coffee. His long brown hair was loose and shaggy. He wore a Dalmatian robe and a raccoon was draped around his shoulders like a stole. He fed it bites of cruller, which the raccoon grasped and ate in tiny delicate bites. The critter froze when he saw us jogging past, and Thor's sonar went up. *I sense the presence of something chaseable.* But when I kept running, so did he.

Seeing Ranger Dave and his critter, I tensed, ready to spring. I cocked my arms back, my strides became jumpy and anxious. Then I watched in what seemed like super slo-mo as Ranger Dave clicked a button on his stopwatch.

Even though I was too far away to hear the noise it made, I heard the click and it sounded like the word *go.* Something shifted channels inside me and my pack and the landscape fell away. I was pure movement, a swift current, strong enough to flow over anything in my path.

Run, Ronnie, run.

And I did. I ran off the bunny carcasses, shredded and

stringy. I ran off our move and my dad's burnout. I ran off Mr. Armstrong's worry. I ran off my own lost hopes of having friends with a future and having a future of my own.

A mile later I stopped and tagged the gas pump at Tiny's Garage, my chest heaving. I brought my sweatshirt up to wipe the rain from my face. I looked above my head. There, with its narrow, twisty shoulders and thundering traffic, was the highway. Trucks thundered past carrying giant logs, mobile homes with bikes mounted on the rear, Audi SUVs with ski racks shedding snow — all on their way back to Portland. But not me. For me, this highway was as far as I could go. Any way further by foot was blocked. And today, like I did every Saturday, as I stood there confronted with my limit, I understood that I ran mostly because I couldn't run away.

༺

Tiny waved to me and flashed me the thumbs-up from behind the counter in his Minit-Mart. I had been speedy, but that didn't matter to me now, because I had to turn around and go back. I allowed myself to trot a few paces, Thor matching me, Trixie and Bailey bounding energetically behind. I would sprint again at the ranger station.

But halfway there, Thor's crooked sonar shot up. He wasn't looking in the direction of Ranger Dave's raccoon — he was looking down the embankment at the river.

I stood next to him and peered over the edge. The noise! It was so loud here! *Lost lost lost* . . . I could feel it building in my head, pulsing, pacing my heartbeat to its own rhythm.

Just below the rapids was a little eddy, a pool no larger than me. There was something sticking out of it, something an unnatural shade of blue. Whatever it was had snagged on a log and was making circles in the water.

I think I knew what it was even then. But I told myself: no. I told myself: it has to be something else. An abandoned dog, maybe. A tire. A canvas bag. A rusty bicycle.

Then I thought: Someone else must have seen this before me. I can't be the first. Even now a competent neighbor is dialing 911. Then I remembered the lackadaisical way Ranger Dave drank his coffee and the thumbs-up Tiny flashed me when I ran past. No one could see what I was seeing and still saunter and sip coffee.

Then I realized: *I* was here. *I* was the help.

I climbed down the embankment, jumped in the eddy and unhooked the blue rain slicker from the log. The body stopped circling and the feet began to point downstream. I put two hands directly under the armpits. What I gripped was cold and sickeningly squishy. I pulled with all my strength. The body was still stuck.

I heaved again and there was a *plop*! Like a suction being broken, and the body came free. I pulled it out of the eddy and flipped it over on the bank.

The scalp on the side of her head flapped, her hair opening and closing like a trapdoor. I patted it back into place because I couldn't look at it. And not because it was gross (there was no blood underneath, only swollen flesh), but because the effect was so awful it looked tacky, like a toupee. Her face was brown with muddy water and I cleaned it off as best I could. Underneath, her features were bloated and pale. Her eyes were open but they weren't looking at anything. Unfocused, they looked like white jelly.

I grasped her wrist, looking for a pulse. Her skin was no colder than mine. I brought my watch up to my face and began to count her pulse. Nothing. I couldn't get a vein. I tried her neck and I still couldn't find it. My hands were so shaky, I was bungling this.

Maybe I should go straight to CPR. I straddled her and pressed my palms into her sternum. Muddy water spewed from her mouth, but nothing else happened. She didn't move; didn't see.

What was I doing wrong? Maybe there was an obstruction. I turned her head to the side, plunged two fingers into her gunky mouth, and pulled out more mud and a couple of pebbles. Still no reaction. I reached further and further back into her throat. I kept thinking: I'm going to gag her. *Come on.* Why wasn't anything happening? Maybe I wasn't using enough force. I pulled my fingers out of her mouth and whacked her on the back, softly at first, then harder and harder. When I finally gave up and let go, she rolled onto her back like a log. Her arm flopped away from her body. It was as though she didn't have any bones.

I rocked back on my heels. I had to be missing something. This was the world's most incompetent rescue. Later, when we were both back at the inn sipping hot chocolate she was going to nail me for sure. Karen didn't have any patience for my City Mouse ways. She would think there was no excuse for not being up to date on my CPR, just like there was no excuse for not knowing which way was north at all times.

I looked up. North didn't help me here, where the trees made a canopy of everything and moss grew on every side of every trunk.

So what was I supposed to do next? I pulled off my jacket and covered her cold body. I was out of ideas. Thor, above me on the banks, had stopped whimpering and was now howling loudly, nose pointed at the low, gray sky. Trixie and Bailey joined in. Behind me, the river's voice swelled. *Lost! Lost! LOST!* The howling and the rapids rose to one giant shriek that made my head throb, and I finally knew, because everything around me told me so, that I had failed.

I took the bank in two leaps. Here was something I could do: I could run. I could get help. Maybe it wasn't too late. I took off past my pack to Ranger Dave's.

I thought I had run quickly before; that was nothing

compared to now. Now I ran so fast and my legs were so cold I couldn't even feel them touch the ground.

I flew.

Even as I ran I knew she was dead, but that wasn't the part that made me hysterical. It wasn't even that the body was small, or that it wore a familiar blue rain slicker: it was the cross-shaped scar on the forehead — the same scar she'd gotten two months ago bouncing on a trampoline by the Kid for Sale sign.

3

There's probably something you should know about Karen, which is that she was mine. Not literally, of course. She was ten years old. I would have had to give birth when I was in grade school.

No, Karen was mine in a way that her brothers and sister were not. She was my guide, and I was her rescuer.

⬡

I first met Karen last August. I'd been living in Hoodoo for three months. Patchworks had been rodent-free for two. Mom's café and the Astro Lounge were already thriving, thanks to a sign on the highway:

GAS FOOD LODGING
CLAIRE SEVERANCE'S
PATCHWORKS INN
3 MILES ➜

That Saturday the weather was still good, the river was low, and risk of forest fire was high. I was a mile into my run when I heard crying. I closed my eyes and the listened. It wasn't the river. The river noise was gentle and atmospheric: the kind of ambient sound you'd hear in a psychiatrist's waiting room. (Unfortunately, I knew exactly what that was like from waiting for my dad.)

No, the crying was coming from somewhere else.

I drew up to the house with the Kid for Sale sign in front and the sound grew louder. We'd driven past this house before. I knew the sign meant *baby goats* for sale, and not the children bouncing on a trampoline in the front yard.

But that day one of them was off the trampoline and wailing in the gravel driveway. She was the source of the crying.

I slowed my pace and walked up to the girl. She was sitting in a heap with her back to me. There was no one else around. "You're okay, right?" I said, more to myself than her. I didn't want to stop — I wanted to keep going. I had no desire to know my neighbors.

Then the little girl turned around, still wailing, and I saw that her forehead was a mass of blood and gravel, drenching her cheeks and pooling in her eyes. I didn't know what to do. I only knew I couldn't stand still. "Stay here," I told her. "I'll be back with help."

I sprinted up the drive to a small red house. The front door was open and I knocked lightly. Inside, a short blond woman was putting away groceries (canned tomatoes, canned beans, canned mushrooms — Mom would have had a fit. Canned beans she could probably understand, but she said canned mushrooms tasted like rubber).

"Excuse me," I said.

She turned to me; her face was thin and haggard, and it fell a bit, as though she knew what I was going to say before I said it.

"I think your little girl fell off the trampoline."

She placed a can on the counter and it rolled off and into the sink. She didn't even notice.

"How bad is it?" she said. She sprinted past me out the door.

"It could just be facial cuts," I said, and even as I said it I knew it wasn't very comforting.

When we reached the girl, still squalling, the mother placed an arm under each of her daughter's armpits and heaved her to her feet. "Let me see," she said, pulling the girl's bangs away from her face. I couldn't help noticing her hair was sticky and didn't come away easily. The kid screamed. "Come on now, hon," the mother said, her face white with anxiety even though her voice was calm and confident. "What would Sacagawea do?"

That seemed to be the magic formula. The crying, which had been pitched to a screech, slowed to a sniffle. Then, without a word to me, the two of them ran back up the drive. *Slam!* The door closed behind them, leaving me out in the cold.

I didn't run again for a moment, just stood there, leaning on the Kid for Sale sign, feeling as though I'd just been Tasered. Behind me, small goats chewed on short, sparse grass. What, I wondered, just happened? Nothing ever happened to me on my run. I was invisible and I liked it that way. I didn't have to smile for the guests, or worse, smile for my parents, who needed me to be okay with the move even though I wasn't.

The next week when I ran past, the trampoline was gone and there was a man standing by the sign. He wore heavy work boots splattered with paint and a flannel shirt rolled up at the sleeves. He looked like a kind but competent woodsman, the sort who could take an ax to a wolf's stomach, or take pity and *not* cut out the heart of a lost and sniveling princess.

"Hey," he said. "Ted Armstrong."

He held a large white paint bucket out to me.

I was pretty sure he was talking to someone else, but there

was no one else around. Just an alpaca in the field across the street eating hay with a great counterclockwise grinding of the jaw.

I took the bucket and looked inside. There was a stack of freshly picked huckleberries giving off a warm, tart scent. Mom would have a conniption over these, putting them into crumbles with peaches or rhubarb or just on their own under puff pastry.

While I was still inspecting them, the man was inspecting his watch. "You're late, Ronnie," he said. "You're usually here at 8:09. It's 8:11."

I frowned and looked up. "How do you know my name?"

The man smiled a kindly woodsman smile. "Are you kidding me? Your mom is big news around here. Everyone knows who you are. We've been watching you run for months."

If he hadn't seemed so earnest I might have been creeped out. But he *did* seem earnest so I decided to cut Kindly Woodsman Guy a break. He was probably just curious.

He continued: "Ranger Dave says your form's good but you're lazy. What do you think this is? A walk in the country?" He chuckled at his own lame joke.

"Who's Ranger Dave?" I asked. I should've thought to ask: and why does he care whether or not I'm lazy? This was before I understood that he was almost as big a celeb as Mom was, not only because of the high-profile rangering,

27

but that in his own day he'd been a world-class runner himself — even trained at U of O with Alberto Salazar — and that he coached track and cross-country at Hoodoo High. But Mr. Armstrong didn't seem to hear me. "Karen! Come say hello to your rescuer."

It wasn't until he called that I'd noticed the kids — the human variety — running around the yard playing something that involved dogpiling anyone who had a ball. From the bottom of the dogpile emerged the little girl I'd stopped for last week. Her clothes were light but sturdy — a T-shirt and shorts. Her T-shirt had a picture of dappled horses galloping past a fence. Her build was that of a kid who'd gotten a growth spurt but hadn't filled out yet. Her knees were knobby and brushed against each other as she ran, her elbows jutted out like chicken bones. She had a blunt brown haircut that reminded me of some guy from a sixties band. A Beatle. A Monkee. A Who.

"Show her your face, hon," Mr. Armstrong said. Karen pulled back her bangs. There was a line of Steri-Strips underneath, making a huge lopsided cross. No stitches. Nothing other than these skinny, transparent bandages which — I'm sorry — *begged* to be picked at. If I were ten years old, I would be hard-pressed to keep my fingers off those things. Let's face it: if I had that many Steri-Strips I would be oozing right about now.

"Do they itch?" I asked.

"Only when I think about it," she said, pulling her bangs down. "You know, in school and stuff. But not around here where there's so much to do."

I blinked. "You're kidding. *Here?*" I said. It just slipped out. There was *nothing* to do out here. Other than run, that is. The boredom was enough to make a person want to learn to appreciate watery beer and date a guy who chewed Skoal.

But Karen looked at me and her brown eyes were afire with enthusiasm. "This morning Kevin found coyote prints. It was so cool. Coyotes usually don't come this close to houses. Come see!" she said, and she reached out and put her fingers in my palm.

Her hand was hot and calloused and dirty. The hand of a kid who didn't mind digging for worms. And yet I didn't pull back.

Mr. Armstrong broke her grip and patted her on the head. "Now now, Karen. What did we talk about? Ronnie has to shave some time off her 10K if she wants to make the cross-country team."

I couldn't help doing a double take.

"I'm not going out for cross-country. I'm just running."

"Uh-huh," Mr. Armstrong said, eyeing me critically. "Tell you what: there's a mile between here and the Ranger Station. See if you can run it in nine minutes. It's slow, but it's a start."

Back off, I thought. If I want to run slow, I'll run slow. But thankfully I didn't say it. Whatever else was up, this guy thought he was doing me a favor by pointing out my faults. Not that I liked being patronized, but he *had* given me fruit.

"Oh, right, the berries," he said, taking the bucket out of my hands. "Leave them here and you can pick them up on the way back."

I considered. I hadn't ever thought about speed, but why not? It was something to do.

I turned to go but then Mr. Armstrong stopped me again. "I almost forgot to ask: could you babysit for us tonight? My wife wants to go to the Tiki Hut for a drink. It wouldn't be long. Just an hour or two. Those pink Scorpion Bowls are really potent. I think they sugar them down." He paused and considered. "Anyway, we don't drink much and the wife doesn't play pool so we should be home by eleven."

My lips were already forming the word *no*. I didn't babysit. Ever. Let alone for four kids. Four kids *without* a trampoline to help them get the wiggles out. What would they have to jump on? Me, probably.

But then a strange thing happened: Karen, the girl I rescued, ran back to join her brothers and sister, but before she did, she waved at me and smiled. "See ya," she said. Her smile was broad enough to melt ice caps. And for the first time since we'd moved, I started to feel at home.

What had her mother called her when she was trying to quiet her? Sacagawea? Everyone in Oregon knew about Sacagawea, the native guide on the Lewis and Clark expedition. She blazed the trail with a bazillion stinky guys in coonskin hats and fringy jackets and no showers and with a baby strapped to her back, too. Without her, Lewis and Clark might have wound up in Peoria.

Karen caught up to her brothers and sister, her face crossed by Steri-Strips that could come off easily in a scrum.

Brave. Very brave. Definitely Sacagawea.

"What time do you want me?" I asked Mr. Armstrong.

∞

In the months that followed I babysat for the Armstrongs once a week officially, more if you counted all the times Karen showed up at Patchworks and wanted to hang out. How could I not? She made everything seem interesting and glamorous. "Hey, Ronnie. The periwinkles are on the move. Wanna come see? Kevin caught this garter snake and put it in his sock drawer. Come on, Ronnie, come look."

I followed as Karen blazed the trail. If she was Sacagawea, then I was Lewis and Clark. I learned to appreciate things other than trash in the ditch. Thanks to her, I learned to spread out fish heads on the back lawn so Fred the Eagle would have a buffet lunch. I was able to pick out jasper and agate from the riverbed. I learned to cast critter prints and take them to Ranger Dave for identification. I learned the difference between petrified wood and plain rock worn into strata by the river. Once, I even found an old flint arrowhead. I gave it to Karen, of course. How could I not? She practically jerked it out of my hands with delight.

All these things we did together didn't have anything to do with Vassar or debate or playwriting or wearing black. They had nothing to do with what I had before and was now lost.

But with Karen it hurt less. What I'd left behind was like my own line of Steri-Strips making a lopsided cross on my forehead. It itched terribly when I thought about it, but with her I rarely did. *How can you possibly be unhappy with so much stuff to do? Come on, Ronnie. Come look.*

4

"Ronnie, what's wrong? What is it?"

I stood heaving on the front porch of the ranger station, my hands on my knees. I couldn't catch a breath. Ranger Dave was standing in the open door. Like the time I found Karen injured in her driveway so many months before, I had trouble forming words, and, like that first time, I didn't need them. Ranger Dave threw on a utility belt with what could have been a gun or could have been a flare over his Dalmatian robe. His movements were deft. This was a man used to dealing with disaster.

"Did you call 911?" he asked.

I remembered the cell phone in my sweats. Why hadn't I thought of it before? I showed it him, too numb and stupid even to press buttons myself.

"Do it now," he said, dashing ahead of me down the porch.

"Do you have a first aid kit?" I found my voice; my heart slowed enough for me to form words. "She's been in the river awhile."

I didn't explain who, but didn't have to. I watched as Ranger Dave's face seemed to catch fire then turn to ash in a matter of seconds. "Make that call," he said ferociously.

He found a kit and sprinted after me as I talked to the "what is the nature of your emergency" operator. I don't remember what I said or what she said, only that I got ma'amed a lot.

We reached the embankment and I was about to sprint back down to Karen, when Ranger Dave threw an arm across my chest. "Stay back," he said. I thought: why? Not like I haven't already seen it. Not like I haven't already fished my fingers around in her cold, slimy mouth. But I did as he said and watched as he clambered down to get a better look.

He walked a circle around her, then crouched low and stuck two fingers into her neck, looking for a pulse.

"I couldn't find the artery," I called down. "And are you supposed to put three fingers or the heel of your hand on the sternum when they're that little? I hope I didn't break a rib." But instead of working on her the way I had hoped he would,

34

he took my rain jacket that was already covering her torso and moved it up over her face. Then he rocked back on his heels. He looked up at me and shook his head.

"Come on," I wheedled. "You can bring anything back to life. I've seen it. *Do something!*"

He climbed back up to the street. "Ronnie," he said, digging his fingers into my shoulders. "I'm sorry."

I wrenched myself away. He had the moist, glassy look of someone who was about to hug me, and I didn't want to be hugged. If he hugged me then somehow that would make it real, and I wasn't ready to give up yet.

"This can't be right," I said. "Karen wouldn't have an accident like this. She's so sure-footed."

"The river changes, Ronnie," Ranger Dave said. "You can't trust it."

I stared down at the body on the embankment. And suddenly the whole horror of it hit me: she was lost.

I started to shake; then I started to snivel. There was some excess snot I couldn't snort back up but had to let drip drip drip into my mouth. Then I gave up trying to contain the runny nose. Soon after, I gave up trying to contain the shakes and let myself rock.

That was when I let Ranger Dave wrap himself around me in a damp hug. And even then I wished he'd leave me alone. All I wanted to do was sink to the ground and curl up into a ball. "You don't understand," I said into his Dalmatian

35

robe. "Who am I gonna follow now? I can't follow her. Not through this."

I knew that was the wrong thing to say but I couldn't keep from saying it. *Me me me.* What was going to happen to *me?* My selfishness just made me cry all the harder. Karen deserved a better friend.

"Shhh," Ranger Dave kept saying, patting circles on my back. "I know. I know."

Then we heard one siren. Two sirens. A whole orchestra. An ambulance came. A Santiam County Sheriff's car came skidding to a stop. Sheriff McGarry herself got out and climbed down the bank. She was a thin woman in her thirties with perfect auburn hair, no flyaways, and she sometimes saluted me when I ran past. If you saw her out of uniform you might think she was harmless and dateable, but when she pulled over drunk drivers she became a grizzly. I'd once seen her approach a drunk coming out of Phil's Tiki Hut, trying to get his car keys to fit into the keyhole of his Chevy. "Sir, will you step away from the car, sir?" When he tried to brush her off she whirled him around and cuffed him in one fluid movement. No matter what the challenge, I'd never seen her rattled.

Until today.

She drew her fingers away from Karen's neck. "God damn, this makes me sick," she said, and pressed a button on a walkie-talkie that was strapped to her collar.

Her deputy, a guy with a top-heavy build and a Fu Manchu moustache, came over to Ranger Dave and me. "Which one of you found the body?" he asked. He had a big, authoritative voice that would've scared me if I could still be scared.

"Ronnie did," Ranger Dave said.

Then the scary man did something that surprised me. He took off his see-through raincoat and draped it around my shoulders. It didn't help keep me dry — I was already soaked — but it was a nice gesture. "I'm sorry you had to see this, hon. We're going to need you to stick around so we can ask you some questions."

I don't like being hon'ed. I find it patronizing. But the way this man said it made me feel encircled, like a jacket. "Thank you," I said.

Then the Lookie-Lous arrived. They must've heard the sirens and all crawled out. I didn't know there were that many citizens in the whole town. Pasty faces; floral print; plaid, denim. Lots and lots of denim. I could make out Casey Burns' mom, in a flannel nightgown and rainboots, a Members Only jacket held over her head like an umbrella. She motioned me over to her but I pretended I couldn't see her. At that moment I hated her, I hated them all, pointing and shaking their heads. There wasn't a one I would trust to lead me through the wilderness.

Then Sheriff McGarry and her deputy put up yellow tape everywhere and made the herd stay corralled, like cattle. A navy blue SUV with "Santiam County Coroner" printed on the side arrived. Someone handed me a cup of Styrofoam coffee, which was how I knew Tiny was there, too. Nobody made worse brew than he did. *He* couldn't even drink it — he called it espresso and charged vacationers five dollars a cup. Ranger Dave acknowledged him with a wave and a smile, but I just looked away. I'd seen enough already that morning.

But I definitely remember the next part, which is that the Armstrongs' truck pulled up and Mr. Armstrong got out.

"What's going on?" He rushed the yellow tape.

"Sir," said the deputy who'd given me his coat. "We're going to need you to get back in your vehicle and go home, please. Let us do our job."

"What job?" he said. "What's happened? My little girl's missing and someone said they thought she might be here."

The deputy looked to me. I nodded once.

He turned back to Mr. Armstrong. "Go on home, sir," he said in his scary, authoritative voice. "You'll be contacted."

"Ronnie," Mr. Armstrong said, catching sight of me. "What's happening? Just tell me: how many stitches is she going to need this time?" He tried to smile but his eyes were bright and watery. He needed reassurance to grasp on to, like a buoy, but I couldn't give it to him.

Perhaps it was then that he noticed the coroner's SUV, because Mr. Armstrong got belligerent. "Let me through," he said to the policeman. "I want to see. I have to see."

"Please, sir, not here," the policeman kept saying.

I shrugged off the Hefty bag raincoat and let it fall to the ground. I marched forward, wrapping myself around Mr. Armstrong the way Ranger Dave had wrapped himself around me earlier. Mr. Armstrong tried to push me away at first. "Get away from me," he said. "You're not mine. You're not Karen. Get me Karen."

But he didn't even try to move, and at last he slumped into me, his body racked with something more than sobs. It was as though huge chunks of him, like embankment, were falling away and churning into the ground under our feet.

Behind us the river was still shrieking; all around us were swollen clouds, making the air so dense we could hardly see, and that was okay by me. It blurred faces and voices. *Sir, I need you to step away, sir.*

I don't know how long I held Mr. Armstrong up. It wasn't long before he was as wet as I was. Ranger Dave offered to shelter us in the ranger station but neither of us let him lead us away. Instead we stayed outside, where a skyful of water, cold as lidocaine, was raining down.

5

After the police were finished with us and the neighborhood gawkers had crawled back to their warrens, Ranger Dave volunteered to drive me home. He had a mud-splattered SUV with these scratchy brown ponchos covering the seats.

By now he was out of his Dalmatian bathrobe and in his beige Forest Service uniform. He left the broad-brimmed Smokey Bear hat at home. "Are you okay?" he asked as I strapped myself into the shotgun seat. The scratchiness of the poncho worked its way through my clothes and into my back and thighs.

I nodded, but both of us knew it didn't mean anything.

Ranger Dave smiled a weak smile, turned the ignition, cranked up the heat, and we were on our way.

Slowly, I began to realize that heat was a very bad idea. The rain-numbness was wearing off and the feeling returning to my limbs. As soon as the feeling came back, so did the memory: that *plunk!* sound Karen's body had made as I pulled it free from the log, the pebbles that had dribbled out of her open mouth when I'd tried to do CPR, the way the side of her head had seemed to open and close like it was on a loose hinge.

It was too hot in here. I couldn't breathe. I was going to be sick. Somehow I managed to get the window down and stick my head out of it, and threw up down the side of his SUV, getting watery vomit all over his Santiam National Forest logo.

Ranger Dave pulled the car to the side of the road and patted me on the back, his hands describing slow circles on my shoulder blades.

"Easy, Ronnie," he said.

I stayed half out of the car for awhile, the rolled-down window practically chopping me in two at the waist. But that didn't dam the flow of pukiness. I heaved even when I didn't have anything left to bring up — just clear, frothy liquid, like whitewater.

"Sorry about your car, I'll clean it up," I choked.

"Don't worry about that, Ronnie. We'll let the rain take care of it."

"She was just a little kid," I said, making no move to get back in the car.

Ranger Dave sighed. "I know," he said, and repeated in a whisper, "I know I know I know."

"The river should be illegal."

I heard Ranger Dave draw in his breath. "Usually I love it. But today I'd fence the whole damn thing if I could."

It was still raining. The back of my head was being pelted and so, with the passenger window open, was the interior of Ranger Dave's car. Those woolen poncho seat covers were going to shrink and smell like moldy alpacas. I pulled my head back in and rolled up the window.

"Take me home," I pleaded.

Ranger Dave nodded and pulled the car back out onto the road.

I leaned my soggy head against the door, miserable. He didn't understand. He was taking me east, toward Patch-works, when I wanted him to take me west, back to my old home — my real home — in Portland.

∞

Believe it or not, I wasn't always this whiny. I used to have things to look forward to — after-school activities where I didn't have to devein anything or shovel anything or grout anything, and friends who weren't already developing beer guts at the age of sixteen.

Before we moved to Hoodoo, Mom and Dad and I lived in a white Queen Anne–style house with purple trim and a wraparound porch in the funky northwest section of Portland, within walking distance of both Starbucks and Coffee People; Cinema 21, and a McMenamin's pub and eatery for when I got tired of Mom food and just wanted a burger. The posters in my bedroom were of Mary McCarthy and Lillian Hellman, neither of whom (rumor had it) liked the other; both of whom were smoking and drinking coffee and wearing black. You could see the depth in their eyes. They hadn't had the easiest, most traditional lives, but they were better artists because of it. They could flay open the human condition and look fabulous while they were doing it. And that was what I wanted. I wanted the sophistication of having many husbands or no husband at all, and I wanted to wear smooth velvet dresses and have deep red, almost purple, lips.

When I lived in Portland, that still seemed possible right down to the accessories.

Back then, my mom had her own cooking show, *The Flowerpot Cheesebread Gourmet*, on Oregon Public Television. She invited local celebs — politicians, Trail Blazers, news anchors, the pygmy marmoset keeper at the zoo — to appear with her and help her shove spicy drumsticks into a tandoori oven or chop cilantro for cool, puckery gazpacho. No one ever turned down a guest spot on her show. She was unfailingly gracious and fed them well.

I used to think of my father as the anti-Mom. He was an attorney with the Public Defender's Office. The kind of guy who used words like *falsify* instead of *fake*. He certainly seemed happy enough, but now I wonder if Dad was ever truly happy or if he was merely satisfied and drowsy, like after a good meal.

Then I woke up one morning and the air was so spicy-sweet I thought it might singe off my nostril hairs.

Mom said the change in our lives wasn't that sudden, and that Dad's break was a long time coming. She said maybe if we'd paid attention to the smaller things, the bigger thing wouldn't have whacked us over the head the way it finally did. All I know is that I will always associate ruin with the sticky-sweet smell of cardamom bread.

∞

One morning last June I woke up at six and could smell the change in the air. I opened my window because inside had become close and airless.

I wandered down to the kitchen where I found Mom and Dad. Mom was wearing her OSU Beavers T-shirt and boxer shorts. Her brown curly hair was winging out around her head, like clusters of purple-black grapes. Dad was in his favorite fleece robe and sitting at the table in the breakfast nook. His short blond hair was matted against his head as though he'd been running his fingers through it for hours.

44

Most of him was pale, but the skin under his eyes was the color of coffee grounds.

I watched from the doorway as Dad buried his head on his arms. "What have I done?" he mumbled. Mom stroked his back and shoved in front of him more cardamom bread, spread thick with honey butter. Then he'd start crying again and Mom would have to reapply her bread cure, like aspirin.

"I don't know why you're taking it so hard," Mom said. "You were just doing your job."

At this point I was tired of lurking in a doorway, so I came in stretching and rubbing my eyes as though I had just woken up.

"Hey," I said. "What's going on?"

The two of them looked up. "Nothing, honey." Mom patted me on the arm and shot me her comforting celebrity-chef smile. "Have some cardamom bread."

Dad sat upright. "That's not strictly correct," he said. "It's not *nothing*."

"Come on, Paul. Stop beating yourself up. This guy was no worse than some of the creeps you've defended."

Dad snorted. "Yeah, well, I wasn't suckered by *them*."

Dad's area of expertise at the public defender's office was guys who were remiss in their child support. Deadbeat Dads, he called them. He said that most of them could hardly be called dads at all. He didn't like any of them; wouldn't invite one home for dinner — a big deal at our house. If he passed any of his ex-clients on the street, he didn't even nod. All my father did was speed these losers through the courts as quickly as he could.

"He acted perfectly normal," Dad said, talking about his latest deadbeat. "He'd been an alcoholic but he'd seen the error of his ways, and with the help of his church he wanted to atone for all he'd done." The oven timer went off. Mom pulled another braided loaf from the oven as Dad picked at the thick slab of bread on the plate in front of him, making tiny efficient crumbs that were perfect spheres, the air squished right out of them.

"I wish you wouldn't take it so hard, honey," Mom said.

Dad pounded his fists on the table like gavels. "Not take it so hard? I helped him get his kids back, Claire. And that guy doesn't deserve to be a parent. You didn't see all the crap they pulled out of that house. There was bleach and rat poison everywhere. Then this whole arsenal. An AK-47 assault rifle in his closet. Pistols, shotguns . . ." He waved his hands around in the air as if he was surrounded by the weapons he was describing, and his only option was surrender. Then he crumpled like a used tissue. "Jesus," he muttered. "There were little kids in that house. Kids that I helped him get custody of."

There were a lot of things about his mini-rant that I didn't understand. I got why firearms made him so uppity, but bleach? Rat poison? Was owning them really a prosecutable offense? What if the guy just had rats and hard-water stains?

Mom looked at me and then looked away. It was just a momentarily glance, but an unguarded one. For that moment she didn't look confident and famous — she just looked tired and old. Then she started moving again. She was a deft cook, braiding and kneading and frosting, but it took all she had just to keep my father from falling apart.

Looking at the two of them should have been my first clue about how my life was going to be from now on: Dad paralyzed by his depression, Mom trying to shield me from it, but incapable of doing so. Her hands were too full. There just wasn't any care left for me.

That morning I sat with Dad until after the sun was up. We didn't talk; we didn't eat; we didn't go to work; we didn't go to school.

"I'm going for a run," Dad finally said, pushing himself away from the table. He stood up and threw away the white peak of used tissues that had piled up in front of him.

Three days later, Dad came home with our new "foster" family he'd repossessed from that last client, over my mother's and my tepid objections. They weren't technically fostered. They didn't take our name and they still had a functional mommy — Gloria Inez, who seemed a fine woman but in need of a job for her green card; and her kids, Tomás and

Esperanza. That was when I learned that Dad's definition of *little kid* (as in "there were little kids in that house with the firearms") included a teenage boy who was six foot six, brawny, and the only Latino I've ever seen able to dunk a basketball. Esperanza fit my expectations a bit more. She was seven, with large, frightened eyes and a thumb in her mouth that never came out.

One week after they squeezed in with us and bathroom time became a commodity, Mom remembered that she'd inherited a run-down inn on the banks of the Santiam River, and wouldn't it be nice to get away? We could fix it up. Only enough to sell it since we never went there anyway.

But when we got there, a change seemed to creep over everyone but me. Tomás relished the room to stretch out. I once caught him standing in the living room, waving his long arms around, not hitting anything, a look of bliss on his face. He was the one who erected a basketball hoop in the parking lot.

Dad ran his hands lovingly over the wooden banisters carved into shapes of animals (brown bears, beavers, herons, eagles) and took over the rain-damaged basement, decorated it with black light posters and converted it into the Astro Lounge. Fixing the tap and filling it with Black Butte Porter, dark and foamy, was the only thing that brought a smile to his face.

Mom and Gloria Inez took steel wool pads to the kitchen

and couldn't seem to stop. At first cooking in the the kitchen was an adventure to them, boiling things over the wood stove and making corn bread in a cast-iron skillet. Then, when that became inconvenient, they started to order new stainless steel appliances and remodeling. There was a walk-in fridge, a gas range with twelve elements, and an industrial-size dishwasher that was so big you could practically drive through it.

Even Esperanza, the small and frightened, wasn't immune to the spell the place wove. She was the one who discovered the stash of quilts that my great-grandmother had made from scraps of gingham and calico. Each blanket was like a map — there was material of cherubic kids kneeling and praying, one of duckies floating in a pond, one of Paul Bunyan with his ax and his big blue ox — all stitched together in geometric patterns with coarse thread. Before we could even have them dry cleaned Esperanza claimed the softest as her own, wrapped herself in it, and plunked herself by the fire.

All of them — they not only loved the place, they needed it somehow. I was the only one unmoved by the tall trees, running water, open spaces, and historic finds. I couldn't wait to get back, and used every excuse to get someone to shuttle me into town. *Please, I can't miss this symphony. Please, I have to go to Lego Physics Camp.* (Never mind that I didn't like Legos.) I was growing frantic, I could feel my dreams being scoured off me with steel wool. All my other friends were going to Avignon to brush up their language skills, to Dartmouth to study with poet laureates, to Salzburg to take violin lessons, or Ashland for Acting Shakespeare 101. All I learned was how to poison baby rats then scoop their corpses out of fireplaces. But who cared what I thought, when you could smell the resin in the air, drink water straight from the river?

Then on Labor Day, Dad decided we needed a weekend getaway every day of the week and moved us there full-time. At that point, all I could do was smile a hollow smile. What was the use of fighting? By that point my old life was already gone, daddy, gone.

But it all started before then, on that sticky-sweet morning in May, with my dad inconsolable and my mother frantically baking. That was when I first sensed life closing in on me. As I sat there in the warm kitchen of our funky urban house, watching my decisive father not know what to do, then finally realizing it was enough to move, *that* was the exact moment I first started running.

6

Mom and Dad were sitting on the front porch when we rolled up. Tomás, my not-quite foster brother, was playing hoops in the parking lot with Casey Burns. They made an odd pair since Casey was a foot shorter than Tomás. But then again, everyone was a foot shorter than Tomás.

Tomás was someone I *definitely* didn't want to talk to today. Don't get me wrong — he wasn't a bad guy. As far as I could tell he was a good kid. He had ways of fixing stuff around the inn before anyone even knew it was broken. But being around him was work. I tried to draw him out when he first moved in but all I ever got for my trouble was a shrug or a "dunno."

I couldn't help feeling sorry for Casey, out here in the rain like a good sport, getting a slam dunk in the face for his effort. But he just laughed it off. Then he saw us climb out of Ranger Dave's car. "Dude, I told you your sister was okay," he said to Tomás.

Tomás palmed the slippery basketball and banked a jump shot, trying to appear nonchalant. But he'd noticed us. "She's not my sister," he said.

"Then why won't you let me . . ."

"Shut *up!*" Tomás elbowed Casey hard in the ribs.

Mom and Dad raced down from the porch. As they did, I heard Tomás spit at Casey: "Do you always have to be *such* a douchebag?"

Dad wrapped himself around me and squeezed hard, like a constrictor, as though crushing the air out of me would make me more alive. I understood, remembering how I'd whacked Karen harder and harder on the back when she didn't breathe. *Violence oughta do the trick.*

"Are you all right, Ronnie?" Dad said. "Dave told us not to come get you."

"You couldn't have done anything, Paul," Ranger Dave said.

"Thanks for bringing her home," Dad said.

"You would've been proud of our girl. She kept her wits and did everything she could."

You can't be proud of me, I wanted to shriek. *I've done*

nothing to be proud of. Oh, man. I definitely didn't have any friendly left in me. Even the word *pride* made me want to smack someone.

"Is it true? Was it Karen?" Dad said.

Ranger Dave nodded.

"That poor family," Dad said, and pulled hard on his face as though he could tug the whole thing off, like a mask.

Mom, perhaps sensing another Dad meltdown, crowded in on me. "Well, at least you're okay, Ronnie. See, Paul? She's fine. You're fine, aren't you, honey?" She nodded at me, willing it to be true. But I noticed her hands were empty. Where were my s'mores? Where was the food that would transform me back into a normal human being? I wanted to lash out at her, claw her eyes from her skull. I wanted to say: *This is your fault. We shouldn't be here at all. You picked what was best for Dad over what was best for me and I'll never forgive you for it.*

But Mom's eyes were so bright and she kept wiping her dry, clean hands on a dirty dish towel. So I just said, "Of course." I tried to keep my voice smooth, without grit. I clomped up the stairs toward the inn, eager to get away.

At the top of the stairs, I couldn't resist looking over my shoulder. Ranger Dave was having a whispering conference with Mom and Dad, and Casey and Tomás had resumed their game. I heard the *plock boing plock boing* of a ball on wet asphalt and then watched as Casey slapped the ball away from Tomás and drove to the basket for an easy layup. Normally, Casey would never be able to get the drop on Tomás, who was as quick as he was tall. He must not have had his mind on the game. Sure enough, Tomás was staring after me even though he looked away when I caught him at it. *Rubbernecker*, I thought. He was a nice guy but no different than the others who emerged from their split-level houses the instant they heard sirens.

I was so busy feeling surly that I didn't pay attention to where I was going, so nearly wiped out when my foot connected with something unexpected. I caught myself on the screen door, then looked down at what had tripped me.

It was the two-by-four with Karen's mud volcanoes exploding with lupine. Only now, thanks to me, they were fully exploded — Mt. St. Helens with a chunk taken out of it. I sank to my knees and hoped I hadn't done too much damage to Karen's last work of art. I started rearranging the lupine blossoms so they were centered, but I stopped.

Dad came up behind me and patted me on the shoulders. "Leave it, Ronnie," he said gently. "Tomás can clean it up."

I turned around. "No, Dad, you don't understand," I said. "Karen must've left these this morning. Should we tell someone? You know, in case she fell in somewhere around here and not downstream?"

He looked at them with renewed interest and started scratching his beard. Not tugging, but scratching. A lawyerly scratch. I could practically see him analyzing it as a piece of evidence.

"Interesting," he said. "I'll show the Brads. You go on in."

With that, he opened the door and shoved me inside.

I stood dripping on the area rug, trying to shake off the excess moisture before traipsing over hardwood floors to get to my room. The Brads? Why would Dad want to tell the Brads about the mud pies?

The Brads were these two blond trust-fund guys — Brad Boyle and Brad Wells, or Good Brad and Evil Brad. They were scruffy, skinny twenty-somethings who weren't interested in anything other than snowboarding and drinking beer in the Astro Lounge. They'd been guests with us since Christmas and showed no signs of going anywhere else, like home or to get a job.

Why would they possibly be interested in Karen's mud pies?

As I stood there dripping, Gretchen came winging out of the kitchen doors carrying trays of brioche French toast stuffed with crème fraîche and strawberries. She was wearing her khaki button-down shirt with the Patchworks logo on it and a white apron. She had brown hair cut in an inverted bob, silent screen star–style, but with a fringe of purple around the nape of her neck. Today she had a Snoopy bandage covering her left nostril, where she'd gotten her nose pierced last month. Mom said she had to cover the hoop while she worked here because it was unsanitary. I didn't think sanitary was the real problem. After all: If you sneeze in the soup, does it matter if your nostril's pierced or not? I tend to think it was more a presentation issue. With Mom, everything was about presentation.

"Hey," Gretchen said now. "We threw out your breakfast burrito. Your mom thought we should save it but I said you probably weren't in the mood for eggs."

"Thanks," I managed. And she was right. Nothing sounded good to me right now, least of all anything runny.

Gretchen balanced the tray on her shoulder, her fingers buckling under the weight of all that French toast. Her eyes softened. "Ronnie . . ."

"Table twelve's waiting for their food," I barked. I didn't want to talk about it. Even with Gretchen.

She narrowed her eyes but didn't bark back. "Right," she said. "I just wanted to tell you I'm sorry. That must've been the most suckful thing ever."

Suckful didn't even begin to describe it but I didn't say so. She was trying to help. It wasn't her fault that every word felt like an invasion to me.

She managed a wan smile. I couldn't help noticing how tired she looked. Even under all the dark eye makeup she had charcoal-colored bags. I looked at my watch. It was now 11:00. She'd been here since 3:00 this morning to start the loaves rising. Baker's hours were always hellish.

"You need to crash upstairs for awhile?" I kept a trundle bed in my room so Gretchen could stagger upstairs when she didn't want to go home. And yes, it was a hotel so she probably could've had a room to herself when it was slow, but it was rarely slow, and Gretchen and I kind of liked being bunkmates. Sometimes we talked about bands or boys at school, but mostly we just slept.

"Maybe later," she agreed. "Your mom wants me to get started on the sticky buns."

"Ah . . . ," I said. Of course. Sticky buns were Mom's grief food. She said that tuna casseroles were overrated and no one wanted to eat them when they were happy, so why foist them on someone who was bereaved? Sticky buns were different. You could eat them and kid yourself that you weren't technically eating, just tearing something off in a long gooey spiral. And oftentimes, Mom said, tearing was just what someone in that situation needed.

"I'll pull out the trundle," I told Gretchen, and made my way upstairs, relieved that I still had the capacity to do something for someone else.

I wasn't kidding myself: giving my friend a place to crash was nothing. It was a small save. Even so, as I walked upstairs, I tallied up the small saves that had occurred this morning. There had been a lot of them: Gretchen throwing out my breakfast burrito, Ranger Dave patting my back as I threw up down the side of his car, Big Moustache Deputy

Sheriff lending me his raincoat, Dad channeling his Inner Lawyer to assess what should be done about the mud pies — even Tomás elbowing Casey in the ribs and calling him a douchebag. Nobody in town had any trouble with the small saves.

It was the larger saves that evaded us all.

7

A shower seemed like the next logical step. Then I would go downstairs to help serve the lunch crowd.

Alas, showering was a mistake. As soon as the hot water hit my back, I realized I'd been getting through the day on numbness. I didn't *want* the feeling back in my skin. I tried to rub it off, loofahing red welts onto my arms and legs, but it didn't make me feel any better. What I'd seen was still wedged tight somewhere, underneath blood and bone.

I came out of the bathroom suited up in my apron and button-down shirt, only to find Gretchen already napping on the trundle. Her shoes were off and her legs were scissored

on top of the covers. Plus she was drooling on my pillow —
the one with the snowshoeing bears pillowcase. She looked
cold but too far gone to do anything about it.

I pulled an afghan up over her. As I did, her hand shot out
from underneath the covers. I thought she might be stirring,
but she merely scratched her scalp, ground her teeth loudly,
and fell back to sleep faceup.

Poor Gretch. I knew lots of kids kept ridiculous hours and
that she needed the money to go to Portland State, but still,
Mom should've had some kind of relief baker so she could
have more down time. Instead, the better Gretchen got at
baguettes and brioche, the more Mom worked her. And
what did Gretch get in return? A dollar an hour raise and a
trundle bed in the Crow's Nest.

There was a knock on my door. "Ronnie! You in there?"

I opened it a fraction of an inch. Brad Boyle was leaning
on the wall, wearing his patriotic bandanna over his spiky
peroxided hair. His nose was sunburned and his lips were
white and waxy with Tiger Balm.

I came out and closed the door softly behind me. "Can
you keep it down?" I whispered. "Gretchen's asleep."

He made an exaggerated shushing motion with his fingers. "Sorry, man. I just wanted to tell you that there's someone downstairs to see you."

I had no idea who that could be. The only people who
ever came looking for me were Gretchen and Karen, and
Gretchen was asleep.

"Who?"

"I don't know, man. Some dude."

"Thanks. I'll be right down."

He looked me over. I was still dripping. "You gonna do something about your hair?"

"Shut up," I said. It was a sensitive issue. I'd inherited my brown curls from Mom, and when I tried to style them wound up with a hair helmet. About all I could do was run a ton of product through them so they didn't frizz out.

He shrugged. Whatever.

I remembered something. "Hey, Brad," I said. "Did Dad catch up with you? He was looking for you earlier."

Brad didn't blink, but a few seconds went by before he answered. "Yeah, yeah. We're late on rent. I told him to charge it to a different card."

"Rent," I echoed, skeptical. Why did Karen's mud pies remind him of that? The logic escaped me. But Brad didn't seem to care if I believed him or not. He slouched off to his home down the hall, the Glacier Lily Suite.

I made my way to the stairwell and stood at the top, curious about who I needed to style my hair for. From my view on the landing I could see Sheriff McGarry and her deputy, the guy who probably wanted his Hefty bag raincoat back, chatting with my father. These guys weren't some dude. Huh.

I was on my way down to find out more, when something occurred to me.

I caught up with Good Brad as he was about to open the door to the Glacier Lily Suite.

"Hold up," I said in a whisper. "Did you see the sheriff?"

He turned around. He'd been talking on his cell and hung up quickly, folding his phone and shoving it in his pocket. It took him a second to compose his face. "Yeah, man. They're trying to figure out what happened to your friend."

"Have you flushed all your, you know, *cigarettes?*"

I hoped he caught my meaning. I never actually smelled wacky tabacky coming from the Glacier Lily Suite. I just assumed it was part of the whole ski bum package.

His smile was faint as February sun and about as vacant. "Don't worry. We've got it covered."

I exhaled. "Okay. Just checking." I turned away. I'd done my part. Now I had a visitor to greet.

"Ronnie," he called. I turned to face him, and was confronted with an expression that was *not* vacant — it was full of weariness and compassion. He took two steps toward me, looking at me so softly he reminded me of Thor the German shepherd. He put a hand on my shoulder, and for a moment the river stopped rushing, I didn't hurt so much, and I realized that whatever else he was, Brad was a decent-looking guy.

He leaned in close and brushed my lips lightly with his own. "I'm sorry about Karen," he said, running his fingers through my damp curls. He patted me once on the arm, opened the door to the Glacier Lily Suite, went in, and closed it behind him.

I stood there looking at the closed door, listening to the low rumble of his voice on the other side. I ran my tongue over my lips. They tasted waxy but minty.

It wasn't a bad kiss, light as a soufflé. And I knew that if I really tried, I could turn him into a knight in my imagination — a hero with no job and spiky hair. But I was short on imagination that morning, and try as I might, I couldn't make the kiss into anything more than it was: a condolence kiss, sincere but meaningless.

So if that didn't mean anything, what did?

We are walking along the riverbank. Karen is leading and I am following. It is a sunny day and the river is low, gentle, and gurgling. Karen is wearing a T-shirt, shorts, and flip-flops. She insists on traipsing through the shallow water in that footwear, arms out perpendicular, as though the slick rocks are a balance beam.

She still has a large bandage on her forehead from her major trampoline bonk.

I watch as she stumbles but quickly rights herself.

Do those shoes give you enough traction?

Don't worry, Ronnie. I do this all the time. Hey, check this out.

She bends over to pick something up. A smooth river rock the color of granite, but round and flat like a pancake.

I lean closer. What is that? I ask. Thunderegg? Agate? Quartz?

Karen shrugs. Just a rock. But watch what it can do. She cocks her arm back and sends that pancake zinging across the water. And even though the river's surface isn't smooth and still like a pond, I can still count the skips easily. One, two, three . . .

Six! That's impressive, I say. Then I add: Isn't it?

About normal, she says. Why? What's your record?

I hesitate.

You don't have a record, she says.

I do so, I say, forgetting that I'm not eight years old.

Hasn't anyone ever shown you how to skip rocks?

No. It's not the kind of talent you can put on your college application.

Karen snickers again.

Could you teach me?

She is reluctant. I am older than she is after all. She leads me in everything, but in this, I have to draw her out. Would this be a good stone? How about this one? I pull a big hunk of something igneous from the riverbed. I toss it, plunk! Like a discus. I think I may have herniated something.

Karen cackles. No, silly, not like that.

She is a great teacher. She has lots of patience, and excellent ways for breaking a huge skill into little pieces: selecting the rock, the grip you need, how far back to cock your wrist, when to use force and when to let go. At the end of the afternoon I am able to squeeze a paltry two skips from a beige stone. Karen and I both squeal with delight.

Then she sends another one that gets eight skips — practically makes it to the other side.

There's a rattling in the bushes over there as something large bounds away. Overhead, Fred the Eagle takes flight from his aerie. We are disturbing things.

I hope we didn't nail any critters, I say.

I doubt it, she says.

Why? I want to say. What's over there? And I know that now, if I ask her, she will ferry me across. But I am still new here and the current, low and gentle as it is, scares me, which is silly. It's just a small river. You can see what's on the bottom. Not like the huge and murky Willamette that runs through Portland. But that one seems different somehow. More predictable. You know you'll get diphtheria if you fall in so there's no mystery to it.

Go on, I *think*. Be brave. Ask her what's over there.

Instead I suggest we go back for cream cheese brownies.

8

Downstairs, I found the café empty. It was early afternoon so the lunch crowd had cleared out. Everyone was either on the slopes or upstairs in their suites. The living room was empty save some guy in a leg cast playing "Kum Ba Yah" on an acoustic guitar. He barely looked up when I came down. He wasn't watching for me, so he couldn't be my visitor, could he? I decided to go to information central, the kitchen, and see if someone there could reveal the identity and whereabouts of my mystery visitor.

Gloria Inez was doing the prep work for dinner, chopping shallots at the butcher block island.

"Hey," I said. "Do you know who was looking for me?" She glanced up, and I saw the family resemblance.

She was a lot shorter than Tomás, but she had the same lustrous lashes, same cliff-like cheekbones. Plus she had this long black hair that, even braided, snaked below her butt. She shook her head. "Are you hungry, m'hija?" She spoke Spanglish with me, ninety-nine percent English, endearments and swear words in Spanish. Tomás spoke the same blend, although he used more swear words.

"No, thanks," I said.

"Are you sure?" She gestured with a huge knife to the warmer where this morning's baked goods had grown cool. "There are Monster Cookies." I looked where she was pointing. A few brioche, a square or two of *far pruneau*, and ah, yes . . . Monster Cookies, big and round as Frisbees. Those were Gretchen's and my contribution to the Patchworks menu, a brainchild from a late night when we were feeling silly and threw everything in the mixing bowl that a cookie could contain: M&M's, oatmeal, butterscotch chips, raisins.

And then I remembered that Gretchen and I weren't the only inventors of Monster Cookies. We had help.

෨

It is Saturday morning. Gretchen and I have been able to grab a few hours' sleep after a late night acting silly in the kitchen. Those giant cookies are sitting on the warmer. We didn't sam-

ple them last night, and now we're afraid. We almost don't want to know what we've done.

Go on, she urges. They look like a great big mess. Mom definitely wouldn't approve because, whether or not they taste all right, they aren't camera-friendly.

You're the baker, I say. You go first.

Tomás comes through the kitchen doors. He staggers with sleep blindness and he's got bedhead so ghastly he looks like a mad scientist. Hey, Gretch says. Feel like guinea pigging for us?

He shrugs and curls his lips. He has a famously bottomless appetite.

I hand him a cookie. He pinches off a corner and chews. This is where we'll find out if these are good or if we should feed them to the Insinkerator, piece by piece.

Well? I ask. Whaddaya think?

He seems to consider. He swallows. He breaks one open and examines the contents.

Needs shredded zucchini, he says. And he has such a straight face that it takes me a while to understand that he's made a joke, and that the cookies are edible.

Gretchen harrumphs. I don't sink so, she says in a fake French accent.

And then a rarity. Tomás smiles. His teeth are blindingly white. If we could just coax him out of the baseball hat, he might be dateable. To someone else, that is. Not us. He has seen us without makeup. We have smelled his atrocious morning breath. He is family.

The swinging doors open with a what what what *sound.*

Morning, slackers, Karen says, taking off her blue whale coat. Where's my croissant?

Gretchen offers her a fragment of a monster cookie. Here, she says. What do you think?

Karen tastes, considers.

Tomás says they need shredded zucchini, I suggest.

He's an idiot, she says. She nibbles again, regards the rest of the cookie Frisbee. Chocolate frosting and gummy worms, she finally says.

Gretchen and I look at each other, and Tomás' smile is blindingly white. Of course. The problem isn't the taste but the presentation, which is Karen's specialty. Dirt-colored frosting and gummy worms are exactly what these cookies need.

Genius, Gretchen says, and breaks out the Baker's chocolate.

∽

I must've been staring a little too long at the Monster cookies oozing gummies, because Gloria Inez sealed the deal. "Please. Take some out. Maybe your father would like one?" She practically worshipped my dad for getting her out of trouble with INS.

I took out a platter and transferred three to them, careful to avoid breaking them. Gretchen must've cooked them af-

70

ter she heard about Karen's death. The gummy worms were out far enough that they flopped whenever they moved, like the real thing. A perfect tribute.

I still needed to find out who my visitor was, and since there was no one else, I approached Kum Ba Yah guy. "Monster Cookie?" I offered.

"Thanks. Maybe later," he said, then went back to strumming. This guy hadn't been expecting me. So who was?

I looked out on the front porch. Evil Brad was crouched over Karen's mud pies. Studying them.

Shouldering the tray, I pushed outside. Evil Brad stood up from his crouch.

I don't know why I thought of him as Evil Brad. He was almost the same as Good Brad — same bandanna around the neck, sunburned nose, spiky hair, joblessness. But where Good Brad didn't mind spending time with us in the kitchen, watching Gretch and me lob raisins into each other's mouths — even joining us on occasion and showing us how to play quarters with a glass of pomegranate soda ("Dudes, you'll thank me when you get to college"), Evil Brad just came home from the slopes and, after feeding, skulked to the Astro Lounge for a microbrew. He treated those of us who didn't drink with contempt.

He barely looked up when I came out on the porch. "Hey, man," he said, scratching his chin, looking at the mud pies. I looked over his shoulder. Why was he interested in those things?

"Monster cookie?" I offered.

He took one from me and bit it absentmindedly. Crumbs scattered all over Karen's volcanoes.

"Dude," I said. "Would you mind not getting crumbs on the evidence?"

"They're not evidence," he said quietly, without a trace of that frat boy accent.

"How would you know?"

His eyes grew wide, then narrowed. It was just an instant, but I thought I could read his expression: he'd betrayed something. I didn't yet know what, and he wasn't about to betray anything else.

He scowled silently. *It's none of your business how I know or why I care.*

I scowled back. "Okay, then, if they're not evidence, what are they?"

And then he stared at me uncomprehendingly, as though I were some kind of primate — interesting but not quite human. "A gift," he said.

And that undid me. Of course they were. A *final* gift.

I was going to puke again. I was definitely going to bawl and I didn't want to do it in front of him. He didn't seem the comforting type. He wasn't a plier of baked goods or a shelterer of injured wildlife or even a consolation kisser.

But I had underestimated him, too. "Hold up," he said, putting a hand on my arm.

"I gotta go," I said, trying to wrench free.

He wheeled me around. I couldn't look him in the eye. I was forced to stand there with my eyes watering, thinking: *This is so unfair. Leave me in peace.* He bent over Karen's art. He plucked the blossoms from each. "The mud won't keep, but here, you should press these in a book somewhere." He stuck them in my apron pocket. "I know it's hard right now, Ronnie, but you'll be glad you did later."

And it was such a kind gesture from such a patronizing swine, that I started crying again.

He pulled the arm of his ski jacket over his wrist and used it to wipe my face.

"Thanks," I said. "I'll pay for dry cleaning."

"No need," he said. He wasn't comforting but he wasn't snide, either. It was just something that needed saying so he said it.

I snuffled once. "I'd better get back inside. You weren't looking for me, were you?"

"Nah, man. He's in the sun porch." The frat boy accent came back.

"Who?"

"How should I know?" he said sharply. "Some dude."

We'd had a moment, but now it was gone, swept down from the mountains and out to sea.

9

At least now I had a place, but no identity. Curiouser and
curiouser. No one ever went on the sun porch. People
couldn't have avoided it more if it were haunted, which was
definitely not part of the remodel.

The idea, when we remodeled, was to screen in the exist-
ing veranda and make it a place where guests could go to
appreciate nature without drowning in it. That was the the-
ory, anyway. There was wicker furniture all around, low
shelves stocked with ancient Nancy Drews, and an antique
Monopoly set, complete with real silver shoe and cannon.

Alas, we'd neglected to insulate, so it wasn't long before

rot and mold worked their way into everything. The ceiling was sprouting black spots that looked like melanomas, the banana slugs oozed in from who knew what crevices, and the smell was atrocious, like rotting fish guts. And no surprise, since guests went there only long enough to strip off their waders or gut their bullhead catfish.

Who could be waiting for me on the sun porch?

I crept up on the threshold and peered inside. I only caught a backpack slung casually over a shoulder, the top of a chestnut-colored head of hair, and I knew.

Oh no, not him. Dread closed in on me quickly, like mold. Good Brad had been warning me about my hair for a reason.

The boy in the sunroom was Keith Spady, my chem partner, who had a very distinctive top of the head. He was the only guy in town with a faux hawk, and he wore it well.

I hung back, peering around the threshold, and took him in. He was examining a sepia picture casually, as though perusing something at a gallery opening. His scratchy army-green Eisenhower jacket was wet, and his Doc Martens were caked with mud.

I had thought, after this morning, that I'd lost my ability to be excited by anything, but seeing Keith Spady on the sun porch sent shivers all over my body, and I liked the feeling. He was braving the smell to see me. As far as I was concerned, that made him a hero.

Once, a while ago, I tried to decide if I was in love with him because he was the only hip guy in town, or if I still would've been in love with him in Portland, a city lousy with boys like that, who listened to the Clash and the Ramones and worshipped Kurt Cobain. I decided I would've liked him anyway because a) he wasn't ashamed of being smart — brilliant at science and math; and b) he had this incredibly enticing tuft of chest hair. It always curled over his T-shirts or plaid button-downs which, on him, looked more grunge than yokel. I couldn't see that tuft without wanting to curl my fingers through it and yank him closer.

He looked up and saw me skulking. "Oh, hey," he said.

"Hey," I said, embarrassed to be caught staring. I tried to recover. "Monster cookie?" I offered, still holding the tray.

He shook his head. "I can't stay. I just heard what happened this morning. I brought you these."

He handed me a bunch of purple flowers. Lupine. Just like the ones from Karen's mud pies.

"Oh man," he said, pointing to my apron, where blooms just like it were poking out.

"It's all right," I said. "I can always take more." I put the tray down and took the bouquet from him. "Thanks. I didn't think these were in bloom yet."

Keith shrugged. "You have to know where to look."

Another explorer. Like Karen.

No. Not like Karen. But still, I wondered if maybe in some weird way, he was here because I deserved him after what I'd been through today. Maybe Keith was my reward for enduring.

I brought the blooms up to my nose.

"They don't smell like anything," he said.

But they did. They smelled fresh, like rain and growth and something more subtle — the promise of spring, maybe? I buried my nose deeper. Not promise; hope. They smelled like hope.

And I could tell, even without bringing the other blooms up to my nose, that they smelled different. Those smelled like courage.

I took in his saturated Eisenhower jacket and muddy Doc Martens.

"You didn't walk all the way here to give me these, did you?" I said. Keith and his mom and stepdad had a hacienda-type house on a hilltop behind the ranger station. They had horses and one picture-perfect golden retriever. So even though Keith's stepdad owned Phil's Tiki Hut, the skankiest bar in the Cascade Range, the LaMarrs lived like country squires. Keith's mom wore bolo ties and expensive belted cardigans made from Navajo blankets, though she definitely wasn't Navajo.

"Nah, I was up here anyway looking for pinecones," he said.

"Pinecones," I repeated.

He peeled off his heavy-looking backpack and unzipped the top. It was full of pinecones, all right. Giant, Ponderosa-sized with lethal-looking points. "Ahhhh . . . ," I said, understanding. I'd forgotten that Keith's mom made "found art" that she sold at the Victorian Cottage on Highway 22. She slapped googly eyes on the cones and put them in various outfits and poses: pinecone with a fishing rod, pinecone on a toilet, pinecone at the dentist. I didn't think that was art, but the asking price was fifty bucks apiece.

"That's great you help your mother like that," I said. And I meant it. I loved that he dressed tough but was considerate of the women in his life. And smelling the flowers he'd brought made me want to be one of those women.

He finally seemed to notice my red eyes and runny nose. Otherwise, why would he have bolted like that? He quickly zipped up his pack. "Gotta run. See you in school!" He took off through the back door, sprinting around the side of the inn like a mule deer, leaving me wondering at what he might've said if I had had straight hair or bigger breasts or more makeup or not been wearing this formless khaki uniform and aerobic-looking shoes.

Instead I was left with another retreating back; another closed door.

☙

I was still standing there when Sheriff McGarry came out to join me, collapsing on the wicker rocker, which listed heavily under her weight. Another thing rotting from the inside. She looked at the lupine in my hand. "Those from your boyfriend?"

I'd forgotten I was holding them. I stuck them in another apron pocket, one far away from Karen's blooms.

I looked up and caught her gazing out the window. She looked tired, the way Mom had that day Dad broke down, and every day since when she thought no one was looking.

"Monster cookie?" I offered.

She shook her head slowly. "Have a seat, Ronnie."

I did, and the sofa groaned under me.

She leaned forward and steepled her fingers together. She did not have a notepad, or a deputy who was scribbling for her.

"How often do you run alone?"

"Every Saturday," I said.

"Do you have a running buddy? Someone to go with you?"

"Not unless you count the dog pack," I said slowly.

She picked something off her lip. "Oh yeah. I forgot about them. Still, maybe you should take someone big with you. How about Tomás? Would he tag along?"

"He's training for the playoffs," I said. "Coach told him

not to work the slow twitch muscles. Listen, what's going on?" I asked. "Why are you asking me?"

She didn't say anything.

And then I knew. In that one, unguarded moment, I could see in her face what had made her so tired.

She didn't think Karen's drowning was just an accident. And now I could see it, too. Someone had made a trapdoor of Karen's hair, and then forced her head under the current and watched her drown.

"Oh my God," I said, puky again. Who could have done such a thing? To *Karen?* And I understood in that moment why people needed to create monsters, vampires and werewolves and sasquatches. It was easier to believe in them than someone with a human face bashing in the head of a little girl.

"Don't jump to conclusions, Ronnie. We won't know until the coroner's report comes back. But I wanted to put you on your guard. If you have to go out and you can't find a running buddy, it's probably a good idea to carry something."

"You mean like my cell?" I said.

She shook her head. "Do you know how to use pepper spray?" She ferreted around her belt and dug something out. A leather pouch that looked like a rustic lipstick holder.

She popped the cap. "Here," she said, tossing it to me. "When you're running, leave it unbuttoned like that. And keep it somewhere handy."

I caught it and examined it. "It looks like Bahama Blast," I said, because that was the first thing my mind fixed on. Pathetic. My only point of reference for a weapon was something you could buy at the Clinique counter.

"Don't point it at your mouth," she said. Then she wagged her finger at me. "And don't be a wuss now, Ronnie. If something happens, use it. Aim straight for the eyes. Don't be a girl and hold back 'cause you're afraid to hurt someone. You use it, and then you *run*. Do you understand? I *know* you can run."

I just nodded dumbly, but she wasn't done with her lecture. "I mean it. Be careful out there. You think this is just a nice little town where people help each other. There's an undercurrent here, Ronnie. You don't know what goes on."

I shivered where I sat. I thought I heard the river wail *monster monster monster.* . . .

"What's happening?" I said, more to myself than Sheriff McGarry.

She sighed, adjusted her polyester pants, and stood up. "I wish I knew," she said. "Now I have to face that poor family. Jesus." I watched as she adjusted her face. All the weariness slid out, and she was once again perfectly poised and composed. She had a job to do.

She walked away and paused at the door. Then, without looking back at me, she said, "For what it's worth, keep an eye on your friend Gretchen. She's on the brink of something, but maybe she can still be pulled back."

I thought of Gretchen passed out on my bed upstairs, scratching in her sleep. What was Sheriff McGarry worried about? Allergies? Overwork?

I wanted to ask her. I wanted to do anything to keep her here with me, because she seemed the only adult who could help me thread my way through this new and nightmarish wilderness.

Instead I let her walk away. She had more important things to do, and the only way I could help was, as usual, letting go and not making a fuss.

I leaned on the door and watched her leave. She stood straight and refused a) crostini, b) crab cakes, and c) gigantic squares of warm corn bread oozing sweet, tart huckleberry preserves. I thought: so much for the cop/donut stereotype. No comfort food for her.

And watching the back of her, stately, responsible, was what finally pulled me out of myself.

Maybe, I thought, the job wasn't damaging her. Maybe it was what was keeping her upright. While the rest of us stood back and offered each other baked goods and flowers and hair advice because we didn't know how to help in any other way, *she* actually had the ability to do something.

I got up off my butt and threw open the door of the sun porch.

I didn't know if Karen's accident had happened up here or somewhere else. I didn't know if it had been "straightforward," or something I still didn't want to face. But for Karen I would face it. *Look, Ronnie. Just look.*

The rain hadn't stopped. Baguette-size patches of snow remained along the yard on the way to the water. Once there, I stood at the top of the embankment, our embankment, which was tamer than the spot I'd found Karen. There were seven smooth river stones forming a stair down to the current. At the foot of them, more stones had been re-arranged to create a gentle pool apart from the rapids. An ancient cedar leaned out, its branches practically begging for a rope swing.

Too gentle, said the voice in my head. Even though I hated everything about the inn, including this yard, it still felt safe.

At Patchworks, a monster was just a big cookie.

I looked across the river, up the river. There were miles and miles of trees that held miles and miles of secrets. The idea of what they might hide scared the bejesus out of me.

Slowly, for Karen's sake, still wearing my white apron and button-down shirt, I turned upstream and began to walk.

The river is slightly higher now. It rained hard for the first time last night, and I'm trying not to think of that as a harbinger. Besides, today is glorious. Hard to believe frost will ever come. It will be summer here forever.

Karen walks ahead of me and volunteers what I wasn't brave enough to ask her before.

She slips off her flip-flops. Come on, Ronnie, let's go see what's on the other side. She puts one foot into the water. It looks cool and accommodating, the way the current flows around her ankles.

I don't know, I say. The rocks look slick.

It's no big deal, Karen says. I've done this lots of times.

The river changes, I say. At least that's what Ranger Dave tells me.

That's what makes it fun, she says. Who knows what we'll uncover? Maybe there'll be cave drawings. . . .

Are there caves over there?

. . . or a new kind of dinosaur.

I know she means dinosaur fossil, but I imagine something huge with big teeth chasing us.

But Karen's eyes are sparkling with the possibility of discovery.

Maybe we'll find a sasquatch, I suggest.

That's the spirit, Clark.

I'm Lewis, I say. Clark was an idiot.

Whatever, she says. Let's go.

Hold on a sec. Wouldn't you rather go for apple cake? It's got caramel frosting.

Swear to Jesus, Ronnie. For a big kid you're a real wuss.

Karen, I say, channeling that stern tone my father uses when he's unamused. We should be getting back.

Fine, she concedes. Run home to the East Coast before we even get to the Mississippi. You're not even Clark.

But she follows me back.

As we turn to go, I watch her face for disappointment. But she doesn't seem disappointed — she seems resolved, and I know that the instant she shakes me off she will cross over, deliberately going farther than before just to prove she can.

If I'm really concerned for her safety, I will go with her now. We will explore together.

Instead I lure her inside my gingerbread house with treats. Come, little girl. Come have some candy.

I know that by tempting her inside I am caging her, and I know what that makes me. She's right: I'm not even Clark. I'm much worse than that. But I still don't want to cross. She'll get over it, I think. She's too resourceful to sulk.

10

That afternoon I barely made it to Clark status. I was a horrible frontierswoman, but I forged ahead for Karen, threading my way through tall grass and Himalayan blackberries, eyes on the banks and on the current. I was combing, a slow walk looking for something someone else might have missed. I didn't find anything unusual — coyote sign (that's what Ranger Dave would have called it — it was really just paw prints and poop), rabbit sign, a hunk of jasper, a thunderegg, and the occasional spent shell casing. I suppose the shell casings were creepy, but even though I was looking for creepy things, I couldn't make myself believe that this was worse than what it was: poaching sign. There were plenty of mule deer with velvety ears and mossy antlers around, but hunting season ended in December. Either the casings were two months old or else someone didn't care about silly little things like hunting licenses.

Ranger Dave once told me that, since it's only legal to hunt stags and not does or fawns, at the first sign of chill, stags will separate themselves from their families, so in case they do get blown away, the women and little Bambis will be safe.

When Ranger Dave first told me that, about the stags wandering off at the first nip in the air to save their families, it broke my heart. But not today. Today there were worse things to be than a lone stag. I'd seen those suckers run. At least they had speed on their side.

Coyote sign; rabbit sign; shell casings. An empty box of Froot Loops circling a backwater. Nothing exceptional. At least not here. But what was on the other side? Ah . . . that would be different.

And yet I didn't even try to cross the river. I blamed it on my shoes with their flat soles. I'd either have to wear them or take them off. Either way there wasn't much safety fording those slippery rocks. I'd seen Karen's scalp. Much as I wanted to help, I didn't want to be another corpse.

I doubt I even made it a quarter of a mile, my frontier skills were so wimpy. Every so often I tilted my head to the rain clouds and said, "I'm trying," as though I were apologizing to a Karen in some heaven in the sky, instead of just around the bend, just out of sight. I told myself that I wasn't looking for Karen herself — I was looking for Karen *sign*. I shuddered and looked at the unknown east bank. Even then I knew that if I wanted to catch up with her, I would have to cross over.

I was saved from a total retreat by a rustling in the bushes. This is it, I thought. Whatever I'm waiting for, it's about to spring on me. I saw a big flash of brown. It was big — maybe a deer, maybe a grizzly, maybe a poacher, maybe a sicko with big hairy arms waiting to force my head underwater.

Step shuffle step shuffle step shuffle. Tomás emerged from a thicket, wearing a brown rain poncho and waving around a flashlight in broad daylight.

"Jesus. You scared the hell out of me," I said.

"You're one to talk. Why did you just wander off like that?"

I didn't know what to say, and muttered something like, "To save the herd," but it didn't make any sense, not even to me. So what? I liked him but that didn't mean I owed him a coherent explanation.

"You really had us worried, you know," he said, and his voice had a cut to it that I'd never heard before, and I was afraid. "You should have told someone where you were going."

And then, even though I'd never even seen his abusive

father, I got an inkling of what he must've been like, because I could see it in the shadows of his son's eyes. This was what kept him quiet around me. This was what he was guarding against. You can't be six foot six *and* mean *and* still hope to have friends. I never asked Tomás how his father was abusive, but I sometimes pictured it when I looked at the giant ropy scar on his wrist. I mean, if you have a father like that, can you ever be mad? Or would you always be afraid of losing control?

But that wasn't the root of the problem. I wondered if he was mad because I was inconsiderate, or if he was mad because he was afraid. I had gone missing the day a body had turned up. "You're right," I said, because he was. And that deflated him. Any hint of rage seemed drain out of him, right through his boots.

"I'm sorry," he said. "We were just really worried, you know. I had to tell your mom and dad that you were off on a lark. And I really *really* don't like lying to your dad."

Tomás practically worshipped my father. He sometimes even let him win at hoops, which did a ton for Dad's nonexistent confidence. It was a sweet thing to watch, if I weren't relegated to watching all the time, wondering how I fit in with them, wondering if I even wanted to. I wasn't a son; I wasn't a sister. What was I?

Water, that's what. Flowing around everything; part of nothing. It was easier that way.

"I'll call them now," I said. I reached instinctively for the pocket with my cell phone in it. But there was no pocket. These weren't my running pants — they were my chinos. Work pants. And I never needed my cell when I was in the kitchen.

"Looking for this?" Tomás asked, and took my phone out of a pocket in his poncho. "Or maybe this?" He took my new lip gloss/pepper spray from another pocket.

I could only look at them dumbly.

"What are you doing out here, anyway?"

I shook my head. "You wouldn't understand."

But then he surprised me. "You guys used to come out here all the time. What are you hoping to find?"

"I don't know. A piece of her, I guess. Just something to show that she'd been here." I meant both on the riverbank and in my life. And Tomás seemed to understand.

"Like an arrowhead," he said.

I reached for the phone. This was a call I really didn't want to make. Tomás was right. My parents were probably freaked. But Tomás held it back, punched a number, and brought the phone up to his ear. "I got her," I heard him say. "Yes, she's all right. It's my fault. I promised her we'd bank-comb. I should've told you. We'll be back in a while."

As he hung up the phone and handed it to me, I felt as though I reached one watery finger through the pane of glass that was still separating us. There were still a lot of things about Tomás that I didn't know, and until I knew them, I wouldn't be his sister or even his friend.

He reached into another pocket, pulled out a flashlight, and pointed it at the banks.

"So what are we looking for?" he said. And that was it. We both had a job to do. But I thanked some unknown deity (in the sky again rather than just around the bend), that Tomás was the one to come get me. I moved over to accommodate, and the two of us had an anti-race, trying to see how slow we could go, and what might be revealed.

It is a chilly fall evening. Karen and Tomás are hanging out, whispering in the kitchen over martini glasses of ceviche — a seafood cocktail in a tangy tomato base. It's Spanish night so there are tapas, salty dishes with olives and Jamón Serrano, and if those don't fill you up, pans of paella to be washed down with pitchers of bloodred sangria.

Mom has hired an acoustic guitarist, a ponytailed guy in a gray vest who is out on the floor right now, his fingers tripping over strings at light speed in a lively but melancholy sound. In a surprise move, Gretchen is doing a table dance, flamenco style. She's had no formal training but she's donned a flouncy skirt and removed the Snoopy bandage over her nose ring. She oscillates like the bread attachment on Mom's food processor. A gang has gathered around her, clapping and shouting E-pa! and trilling their tongues. Ai-yai-yai!

Back here in the kitchen, which smells of saffron and capers,

Mom has complicated our lives by insisting on serving ceviche in martini glasses. I've already broken three, they're so top-heavy, they tilt at the vibration of a guitar string. But Mom says the stemware is necessary because it makes the shrimp and squid ring look classier, and she's right.

Karen and Tomás are leaning against a butcher block. Karen is forking calamari from her top-heavy glass with a plastic cocktail sword. She is a third of Tomás' height, even when he's slouching. She nudges him in the thigh and nods at me.

Hey, guys, I say, unloading dirty dishes in the sink.

Order up, Mom says. I reload for table seven.

Hey, Ronnie, Tomás says, straightening to his full, lurching height. Do I notice him? Or do I notice Karen stamping hard on his foot? Hard to tell. It's just a rustling in the corner of my eye as I pile plates on my tray, trying not to tip the ceviche glasses.

Are you coming to the game on Friday? Tomás says.

Of course.

I go to all his basketball games and sit on the bleachers between Esperanza, his little sister, and my dad. Dad jumps up every so often to get us nachos with Squeez Cheez and stale donuts and root beer from the marching band concession stand. He always looks guilty as he does it but I don't care. In our lives, stale, processed food is a rare treasure — an elaborate quartz in the middle of a brown thunderegg.

Now, in the kitchen, Tomás looks to Karen, who gives him a "go ahead" motion. She even kicks him in the shins.

Great, he grunts to me. Maybe . . .

Veronica? Mom calls, shaking a curl out of her eyes. Her face is flushed with heat and stress. We have paying customers. I've got to get this food to table seven.

Gimme a sec, I say to Tomás, and balance my tray carefully out the kitchen doors. No ceviche spillage this trip. Score one for me.

When I come back in, I am ready to hear what he wants to tell me. I'm about to tell him okay, I'm here for you, at least until I have to jump up again, which is going to be instantly. I know I'm technically an only child but I'll be Marcia Brady to your Greg. Together we'll put the blend into blended family.

But when I back through the swinging doors, I see something that unsettles me. Karen is reaching up to poke Tomás in the chest.

You may look like the Hulk, she says, but you're just a giant sissy. She spits with accusation. Tomás shrinks where he stands. At that moment Karen is taller than he is.

When I ask him later about what he wanted to say, Tomás tells me it was nothing. When I question her separately, Karen also says it was nothing. But I can't shake the feeling that, had the joint not been so busy at that particular moment, the two of them would have outflanked me in some way.

11

Tomás and I got back from our bank-combing at twilight, what should have been the beginning of the dinner rush, but no one was rushing. As we stood on the sun porch shaking ourselves off, I took in the changes. Mom had set up warmers of food along the café windows. Odd. Mom didn't believe in buffet-style meals. She said they were salmonella in the making, a sign of a lazy chef serving egg substitutes and near-bacon on Sunday mornings.

And then, next to the sun porch door, was a stockpile of things — chanterelle mushrooms in paper Safeway Foods bags; jars of blackberry preserves and spiced peaches, pickles with a label that said "Aunt Irma's Private Select" on them. And it wasn't just food in the stockpile. There were hand-knit caps, mohair blankets, ancient videos of Babar and Dora the Explorer — all collected in a giant wicker basket, beneath a sign-up sheet that said "Armstrong Babysitting Rotation" at the top.

The list was completely filled with names.

"What's this?" I asked Tomás, tapping the paper, which was only beginning to curl upward, like a scroll.

He shrugged and stomped the river water from his boots. "Just what it looks like," he said. I couldn't tell if he was being sarcastic and didn't get to ask him before he tromped off into the kitchen.

I studied the list again, then peered through the sun porch window. The whole first floor was completely full. I don't know what Mom had in the warmers but people were eating it — some of them off paper plates balanced in their laps while they sat on sofas. Mom didn't believe in paper plates, either. Kum Ba Yah guy was still there, but he had progressed to "The Long and Winding Road." No one was singing along, but no one was gossiping, either. The mood — at least what I could see from the sun porch — was somber but respectful.

"It was smart, really, bringing everything here." Dad was leaning against the doorjamb, two fingers loosely gripping the neck of a Pyramid Hefeweizen. "They all said the same thing. They wanted to bring tuna casseroles to the Armstrongs but thought your mom would be a better person to coordinate help."

Looking at those people through the window made me feel the way I had shoveling that bunny carcass while everyone was warm and inside: I was circling something, looking for a way in. So I rallied the best way I knew how.

"I'm ready to work," I said.

"You don't have to if you don't want to," he said. "Gretchen and Tomás and Gloria Inez can cover, if you need some time to yourself."

I tried smiling at him. "If it's all the same to you, I'd rather keep moving."

Dad smiled back at me, and it seemed the smile even reached his eyes, as though to say he knew exactly what I was talking about. Then he reached into his pocket and pulled out a green plastic pill bottle. When he shook it, the contents rattled. "Before I forget, have you been in my medicine cabinet?"

"No." I stayed away from Dad's pharmaceuticals, convinced they were the only things keeping him from mildewing and curling up on himself. I had Advils for the days I worked out too hard. That was as serious as I wanted to get.

" 'Cause I thought I had twenty of these but now there are only fifteen."

"Fifteen of what?"

"Lorazepam," he said, twisted the cap off, shook out two,

and handed them to me. Since my hands were still wet they left little chalky circles in my palm.

"I'm not sure I want these," I said. The way he hoarded them made me deeply suspicious.

"Nothing to be afraid of, Ronnie," Dad said. "I take them sometimes to help me sleep. If I've had a really rough day. You know. Like you have."

I doubted he'd ever had a day like mine in his life, but maybe he had. Maybe that was his problem. Maybe at his old job, he had them five times a week, fifty-two weeks a year.

"Take them one at a time. They're addictive. And any analyst will tell you that what you're feeling now — eventually you have to let yourself feel it. That's when your mother's talents come in handy. Pain is a lot easier to take with a meal."

Like asprin, I thought, looking at the teeny pills in my hand.

Dad smiled sadly at me and walked away, skulking back down to the Astro Lounge. I assumed that was full of informal mourners, too.

Even though he told me I didn't have to pitch in, I spent the evening circulating among customers, helped bus paper plates, all the while listening to snippets of conversation. People were sharing memories of Karen, as if sharing was a way to hang on to her. They all smiled warmly at me and some even gave my hand a squeeze, but no one questioned me — not even to ask how I was doing. It was as though they'd all resolved to let me be. And I felt a kinship for all the generous souls in that room, with their woven memories and crocheted hats and their soft but firm grasps.

"I had her in Sunday school, you know," I heard one blue-haired woman say to another. "She couldn't have been more than five. She asked me if elk could get into heaven. I tried to tell her that they didn't have souls but that didn't seem to help. Poor thing. She must've seen one strapped to the hood of someone's pickup."

The other blue hair clucked sympathetically. "That's a toughie, all right." They themselves seemed perfectly at home with the soul/no soul delineation. I envied them their sureness. Me? I didn't know what I believed. If elk didn't have souls, what about well-loved household pets? Dogs who wore bandannas and caught Frisbees; cats who purred and kneaded your lap when you watched *Gilligan's Island* reruns; and maybe even goldfish who swam up to you and smiled when you walked toward them with fish flakes. Didn't they deserve souls if we loved them enough?

I ghosted around until the end of my shift, my gestures practiced and fluid. I didn't work so much as drift along, contemplating the big questions. I didn't make any progress. At the end of the evening I'd circled around the afterlife more than the buffet. Finally, around 11:00, after the joint had emptied out, I went upstairs and collapsed on my bed.

Gretchen had neatly tucked the hide-a-bed back underneath so there was no evidence she'd been here at all. She was a really good bunkmate.

I remembered Dad's pills and pulled them from my apron. They were so teeny. Could something so small really pack a big wallop?

I put them on my nightstand. Maybe as a last resort, I thought. Besides: Dad had said that eventually I'd have to feel the pain. Why not now? No sense putting it off. Maybe I didn't need them to get to sleep. Maybe all I needed was a soundtrack.

I know it's weird, but nothing relaxes me so much as a band with really loud, really driving guitars, like the Clash or the Ramones. Or sometimes, if I'm feeling really low and deep, like I was tonight, I would reach even further back into the history of pop and go for the Who. Not just any Who. It had to be *Quadrophenia,* one of Pete Townshend's concept albums, like his rock opera *Tommy.* I didn't know what "concept" meant, other than the whole thing was supposed to stand as a whole instead of separate tracks plunked together. There were common melodies running through-out — some of them so subtle they sounded like echoes. Like: "Is it me, for a moment?" *Moment moment moment . . .* There's a movie *Quadrophenia,* too. It's about this kid who does too many drugs and feels like there's a separate him for every occasion. Major identity crisis but since he's English, he may feel divided but looks super spiffy with his rain parka, tooling around on his Vespa. At the end of the movie he stands on the seat of his scooter, kicks it into gear, and drives it off a cliff. You see it crash onto the rocks of a shoreline a hundred feet below, but you don't see his body falling with it. And that's the end of the movie. As the credits roll, you're left to wonder: did he really do it? Or did he chicken out at the last moment and decide to live?

That last part was certainly morbid. But suddenly nothing else would do. I had to listen to *Quadrophenia*. I couldn't go to sleep without it. Luckily, I had the whole thing in my iTunes.

I pulled open the drawer to my nightstand to fish out my iPod, but it wasn't there. I foraged for it under bookmarks, a diary I never wrote in anymore, and several highlighters which, before they'd dried up, were pink and yellow. No luck. Then I thought: maybe I left it in my backpack. It wasn't there either. Nor was it in my desk or on my bookshelf or hidden beneath the pillows on the window seat. It wasn't in the bathroom. (I didn't think it would be, but I was so desperate I checked anyway.) Finally I decided that there was nothing I could do. I'd look in the kitchen tomorrow, and then my school locker on Monday. *Quadrophenia* would have to wait.

I put on my jammies and crawled under the five layers of quilts. I thought about reading for a while, but then took another look at the two tiny pills on the nightstand and thought, do I dare?

There were more ways to be brave than crossing a swift current. So I scooped one of the pills up in my hand, stood on my Vespa, and jumped off a cliff.

Lost lost lost . . .

I am back on the Santiam River Road with all its twists and turns. The sky is overcast. Around me giant fir trees weep moss; the river wails as it rushes past. I am running toward the inn, but not gaining any ground. It is like running on a treadmill made of quicksand.

Then I round a bend and see Karen alive, wearing her blue whale slicker. Her light brown hair falls in perfect ringlets, but when she turns to me I see that the scar on her forehead is bleeding. Bright red blood and gravel are dripping into her eyes the way they had the first day I met her.

Karen! I call. I have to get to her. Something terrible is going to happen and only I can stop it.

She runs away giggling.

I run after. If I can catch her, I can save her. But no matter how fast I run I get nowhere.

Wait! I call as she disappears around yet another bend. Come back!

She pushes open the iron Patchworks gate and my heart leaps. Patchworks is not her destination. She is going beyond, and if I don't get her back now, she will always be out of reach.

I sprint as hard as I can. I have to stop her.

She pauses on the back lawn, where gray river rock meets lush green grass. She kicks off her boots.

No! I lunge for her feet, raking at her with my fingernails, trying to drag her back.

But I am too late. The river floods the banks, its crying now a raw wail.

Lost! Lost! Lost!

12

When I awoke after what felt like only five minutes of sleep, it was still dark. A little girl with brown hair was leaning over me.

"Ronnie? Are you awake?"

My first thought was: Of course she's still alive. Yesterday was the nightmare. Then I floated completely to the surface of my mind and remembered that that was impossible, and I jumped upright and crabwalked as far away from the apparition as I could. I could feel my fingernails oozing blood as I gripped the sheets. I'd clawed them raw, trying to drag Karen back in my nightmare.

The apparition before me now didn't say anything, but neither did she disappear. After a few minutes, when my heart stopped sprinting, I reached over and switched on my bedside lamp.

"Jesus, Esperanza. You scared the pants off me. I thought you were a ghost."

Esperanza's lip wavered and made a kind of cedilla shape under her mouth. That was one thing she had in common with Tomás — both their expressions looked like punctuation marks. I wasn't concerned about the cedilla shape though, because it almost always looked like that. She was sensitive to the point of an anxiety disorder. Which meant that other than the passing physical resemblance between the two girls (brown shoulder-length hair, rounded belly of puppy fat), she was in fact the anti-Karen. Besides, Karen was ten and Esperanza was seven, which didn't seem like that big a gap, until you factored in that while Karen knew how to identify every species of plant and rock this side of Dufur, Esperanza's lone talent seemed to be sucking her thumb. It was a habit no one tried to break her of, everyone's attitude about it being: why not if it gives her comfort? She's had enough upheaval in her life.

"What happened?" I said.

"I couldn't sleep."

"Where's your mom? Where's Tomás?"

"Asleep."

"Ah," I said. And really, it made a strange kind of sense. But still. "Why wake *me?*" I asked her.

"Because I'm afraid," she mumbled, her eyes flicking around the room.

"Of what?" I said.

"*La llorona,*" she whispered, as though even saying the name gave it power.

As I may have mentioned before, my Spanish is limited to what I heard Tomás and his mother say, which, in Tomás' case, was mainly swear words.

But when Esperanza said *la llorona,* I suddenly felt cold, as though a freezing wind had whistled through the eaves and entered my bones. I didn't even know what it was and I was afraid, too.

"What's a *llorona?*"

"The river spirit," she said. "The crying woman who drowned her own kids and lives in the water, waiting to lure more kids to their deaths."

Lost lost lost . . . The crying woman. A water spirit. Was that what I had heard wailing to me this morning, before I knew anything was wrong?

I took a deep breath. "Who told you about that?"

"Mamá," she said.

That didn't seem right. I couldn't imagine Gloria Inez intentionally freaking her daughter out. She was too capable for that.

"Really."

Esperanza twirled her hair nervously and wouldn't look me in the eye. "I heard her talking to Tomás. They didn't know I was listening. Tomás was trying to tell her that *la llorona* was a fairy tale but Mamá said there are hungry spirits all over Mexico, so why should it be any different here, just because it's colder?"

I wiped the crust, thick as cornmeal, from my eyes. "I see."

She looked up at me. "What do you think? Is *la llorona* going to come for me next? That's what Mamá thinks. She told Tomás not to let me out of her sight."

I knew what my eyes and ears told me, which was that the river was hungry, and that it would swallow all of us if it could, starting with the ones least able to defend themselves. But I also wasn't about to tell that to a little kid. Especially one as squirrelly as Esperanza.

"There's no evidence for that," I said. "Look: Karen's death was an accident. She slipped on a rock. It's easy to slip. I know. I've done it. This was a tragedy but nothing more. I wouldn't worry about some spirit that lives in the river waiting to devour little kids. *La llorona* doesn't exist."

I didn't believe what I told her, but I sold it. I don't know if it was my delivery or if Esperanza just wanted to hear the words, but she seemed to relax. Together we pulled out the trundle and slammed it next to my bed. She peeled back the covers and crawled in. Then she reached over to my nightstand and withdrew something from the top of a stack that hadn't been there when I went to sleep. "I brought some books," she said, tossing one in my lap. "Read," she commanded, then stuck her thumb in her mouth and twirled her hair.

I cracked open the first book and did as she ordered. She'd selected all stories about monsters with gnashing teeth and terrible roars, but were easily controlled by one gutsy child. And it gave me hope. If she'd wanted to read about fairies or princesses living a sparkly-shiny existence, I would've been worried for her. But maybe if she could read about being gutsy, then one day she would find the strength she could only now read about and suck on.

Finally, when the last monster was vanquished, her thumb slid out of her mouth and she fell heavily against a pillow, leaving a line of spittle on the sham with the antique duckies. I reached over her and turned out my lamp, telling myself that there was safety in numbers, and that maybe *la llorona* wouldn't get us as long as we stuck together. But outside my window, the river didn't care.

Lost . . . lost . . . lost . . .

It was a horrible lullaby and I knew my brave words had no power over it. It may have made Esperanza sleep easier thinking we were an army of two, but I saw the truth: we may have been an army of two, but one of our ranks still sucked her thumb.

The next time the river jumped its bed, I was our only defense.

13

Hoodoo High stood on the banks of Detroit Lake, the body of water that the Santiam bled into. Beneath the lake was a series of dams, and beneath that the Willamette River, which fed into the Columbia. Or the "Mighty Columbia" if you're a victim of educational films about the Landscape of the American West, blah blah blah. If you bought into that kind of regional-speak, the whole state was Mighty. Mt. Hood was Mighty, Smith Rock was Mighty, the winds that whipped through the gorge were Mighty. The only thing in the state of Oregon that wasn't Mighty was the Hoodoo High mascot, the Hodag.

At one point in its evolution the Hodag was probably Mighty, too. He was a frontier tall tale, a lot like sasquatch. He was supposed to be a giant furry dragon, a menacing demon who lived on Hoodoo Butte, lying in wait to trip skiers and shred their rotator cuffs. Alas, the Hodag depicted on our Hoodoo High walls was too cuddly to be fierce. He looked like some character from a preschool cartoon: Nonthreatening Animals from Mythology Who Eat Cupcakes and Make Macaroni Art.

Gretchen and I shared a locker but our schedules were so different we rarely saw each other until our last class, chemistry, which I sucked at. Wrong side of the brain; too much memorization.

Still, chemistry was my favorite subject at Hoodoo High because of Keith Spady. And after my embarrassing breakdown in front of him, I was hoping to make up for it. The least I could do was wear a low-cut T-shirt. I wasn't sure that would help, though. I'd had mosquito bites bigger than my breasts.

When I pulled up a stool in chem on Monday, Keith wasn't there yet, but Gretchen was, sitting kitty-corner from me at our workstation. Her head was on her desk. She was power napping again.

"Gretch?" I ventured quietly as I sat down.

She bolted up, as though she'd been zapped by something. "Oh hey," she said. There was no Snoopy bandage on her nose today, so her pirate-style nostril hoop was clearly visible. She gave her scalp a good scratch.

I remembered Sheriff McGarry's warning about her being on the brink of something. I wished I knew what. It was there, in the itchiness and the napping and the blankness of her stare. They were a formula I couldn't quite make out.

"Do you need an antihistamine? I bet the nurse has some."

She ogled me as though I were speaking another language. "You're itching a lot," I said.

She brought her hand down and examined her fingernails. "Oh yeah, that," she said. "I've got a hot spot. Good thing it's not in my nose. God forbid I should be unsanitary." She smiled and I smiled along with her, but I was unsatisfied. Her eyes were bright, and her words had a polish to them, as though they were scripted. It was almost as though she were expecting me to ask her about it.

Then Gretchen's eyes focused and she stared over my shoulder at the door. "Oh geez," she said, and sunk into her stool, her arms crossed.

Keith Spady. I didn't even have to turn around to know it was him, because you could smell him from halfway down the hall. He'd been smoking cloves again. He was the only one I knew who engaged in that particular spicy-sweet vice. It was comforting. Like cardamom bread.

I ran my tongue over my teeth hoping I didn't have anything left in them from lunch. I studiously did *not* look at the door. "Ah, Jesus," Gretchen groaned when she saw Keith. Then she hissed at me: "He can tell, you know."

"Tell what?"

"How into him you are. Please. Have some dignity. His head's already big enough."

But when he pulled up a stool and sat down beside me, my head throbbed from excitement and misery. There was that curl of chest hair, there were the hip clothes. As any English-concept-album junky could tell you: wardrobe makes a difference — even on a guy. And Keith dressed as though he'd just stepped off the set of *Quadrophenia*.

He plopped his books down on the counter with a loud thunk. "Gretch, I've been thinking. You should have a party," he said, talking across the table.

"*What?*" Gretchen said, outraged, and I got a whiff of something stronger than clove cigarettes. Gretchen not only didn't like him, she *hated* him, and I couldn't understand why. After all: they were the only two hip people in the school. You would think they would get along. But Gretch clearly didn't want to have anything to do with him.

"Party," Keith repeated. "And here's why: Ronnie needs to cut loose."

"Huh?" I said. He hadn't discussed this with me. He hadn't discussed anything with me ever. Except pinecones. And the periodic table.

She shook her head and she looked sad. "Don't drag her into this," she said.

"Into what?" I asked, but they didn't seem to hear me.

"Come on. Nothing helps you get over an untimely death like a kegger."

I could only stare. I couldn't decide if he was so cool I couldn't even comprehend him, or if he was just an insensitive clod.

Gretchen had no trouble deciding what he was. "No," she snipped. "Definitely not." The atmosphere changed with Gretchen's short words. It was as though before she spoke the air was soft and fragrant, and afterwards lopped, as if she were trying to slice him off like pinwheels of cinnamon dough.

Luckily Keith wasn't so easily lopped. "How 'bout Friday?" he asked.

"Friday's no good. Mom's got the night off."

Gretchen was a latchkey child. We had no idea where her father was, and her mother, Mrs. Kinyon, kept hours that were almost as bad as Gretchen's. She waited tables at Phil's Tiki Hut, which made Keith's stepfather, Phil LaMarr, her mom's boss — a guy with a gray ponytail who sported various flavors of Hawaiian shirt: hula girl, palm tree, mai tai, hula girl, hula girl, hula girl.

"How about Saturday? I'm sure she's working Saturday. I can con Phil into adding her if she isn't already on the schedule."

116

"Keith, you know I don't like this," Gretchen said. But what she was really saying was: *Don't ask me one more time because I'll agree to it and I don't want to.*

Keith snorted. "A little late to be playing innocent now, don't you think?"

Gretchen's eyes fell to the floor. I still didn't know what had happened between them, but it was enough to take the snap right out of her. That didn't seem right. True, the way she dressed and talked made you think that she was tough, but still Keith had stung her. If I wasn't so into him, I would've kicked him in the shins.

It took me an embarrassingly short amount of time to forgive him for everything — his jab at Gretchen, plus his crass idea that a party might help me forget Karen. I told myself: some cool guys were just that way, and putting up with it was the price you paid for basking in their aura.

"If you think a party is such a good idea, why don't you have one at your place?" Gretchen had gotten over her shame and was rallying.

Keith shook his head. "My mom would never go for it. She's different from yours. She's really into her stuff."

I assumed he meant the pinecone art.

"My mom's into her stuff, too. She just has less of it," Gretchen spat.

Gretchen and her mom weren't exactly trailer trash but neither did they live on a hilltop and keep horses, the way

117

Keith's family did. Gretch and her mom lived in a two-bedroom rambler across the street from the Armstrongs. Gretchen kept it immaculate. There were always notes from her mother on their kitchen counter that began with "Gretchen — I want you to . . ." followed by lists that usually included vacuuming and making shortbread.

"Look," Keith said. "That little kid would want you to have fun."

"Her name was Karen," I said. And, rock star or no, Keith was beginning to bug me. Could you hate someone and want to wrap yourself around him at the same time?

"How do you know what she'd want?" Gretchen added. "You didn't know her."

It was my turn to shrink on my stool, content to let Gretchen navigate for me. I didn't even want to stick my toes in this one. It was treacherous, full of something submerged and slippery. On the one side, there was Gretchen staring at me, silently ordering me to back her up in the name of righteousness and friendship. And on the other side, there was Keith, confident, abrasive, equally sure I would back *him* up because he knew I was crazy about him. But I knew this wasn't about me. Or Karen. Or beer. There was something else going on between them, something that made Gretchen scratch even more furiously and Keith strut with conceit.

Then Keith laid a hand over mine. "If you're there, I'll be, too," he said. And the expression in his eyes was so soft that I didn't care if Gretchen and I were being played or not.

"It isn't right," Gretchen hissed, mindful that she'd lost before I even said anything. "You know it isn't, Keith. I don't care what Ronnie says."

"Come on, don't be a sore loser. Look at you two. I've never seen a pair more in need of a break than the Patchworks Twins."

I'd never heard us called that before, but it seemed right. It made me feel jagged and wobbly, like a scarecrow, all straw coming out of burlap, but bound by coarse thread to someone else who was equally jagged and wobbly. Between the two of us, maybe we could stand straight.

But not now. Gretchen put her head on her desk and even banged it once for effect. "All right," she said, her words muffled because she spoke them into the Formica worktop.

Keith withdrew his hand from mine. "Yesssss. Thank you very much." He pumped his arms in the air and glared triumphantly at Gretchen as though he'd just treated her to a giant slam dunk in the face.

"You'd better help me clean up afterwards, Ronnie," she said, her anger still carrying her.

"Of course," I said. I had no problem with cleaning. I cleaned up plenty. Only not at Gretchen's house, which I tended to look on as a Ronnie sanctuary, where I could drape myself like wildlife over the living room furniture and listen to her CDs and watch her TV while she vacuumed around me.

But right then I would have mucked out her toilets because of the way Keith put his hand over mine. Saturday was definitely it. He as much as promised it with his eyes. This would be the weekend things changed between us.

I must have gone back to gazing at him dreamily because Gretchen caught me and shook her head sadly. *Let it go.* But there was no way. Because being next to Keith made me feel substantial in a way that nothing else did — not even running. I was tired of ghosting around. I wanted back in my own flesh, and nothing did that to me like the promise of running my fingers over his stubbly Adam's apple and kissing his spicy-sweet mouth. I could practically feel him pressing against me in an embrace or a slow dance, and I wanted it. At that moment I would've snuggled up to the devil himself as long as he made me feel alive.

14

After the last bell, Gretchen and I retreated to our locker. She bused it home in the afternoons and Tomás and I drove together, hours later, after practice.

Tomás was already at our locker now, wadding up pieces of notebook paper and lobbing them, jumpshot style, into a trash can. I couldn't help noticing his grace and upper arm definition. He seemed, as always, like the opposite of quick. He seemed to be moving so slowly, it was as though he were jumping under water. But each trash can shot went in.

"Are you behind the three-point arc?" Gretchen asked, fiddling with the combination lock.

He appeared to consider this. "Nah, that's the cafeteria," he said, and his face was so serious, it took me a second to realized he'd made a joke.

He turned to me. "So when are we going out again?"

Gretchen looked at me and her lips curled into a sly smile.

"It's not what you think," I said.

"Ronnie and I are just exploring the river. You know, the way she used to do with Karen?" And this made so much sense I wanted to smooch him. He didn't say *Ronnie's deranged* or *she needs closure so we have to humor her.*

Gretchen wrestled textbooks into her backpack. "You're kidding, right?" she said. "It was an accident, Ronnie. Let it go."

I sighed and retrieved my gym bag. I didn't want to let it go. Letting go meant having everything that I loved about Karen drift out to sea. I wanted the opposite of letting go. I wanted to grip her memory so hard I could haul Karen herself up out of her fate. "Whatever," Tomás said, communicating with the curl of his lips how unfazed he was by her opinion. "I take it you're not coming with us."

Gretchen slammed the locker shut. "No, I am not because the whole thing is ridiculous. Do you have any idea what you're looking for or where to look?"

I shook my head.

"And even if you did, it's been pouring buckets for the past three days. Don't you think if there were any sign of what happened to her it would be washed away by now?"

I didn't have an answer. Tomás just stuck his hands in his pockets and scuffed the floor. Talk about pouring buckets. She'd just dumped a reservoir on my state of mind.

It must've shown on my face because Gretch let out a sigh that sounded a lot like a huff.

"Listen, Ronnie," she said. "I know you're hurting. But what you're thinking about, it's too futile. There's got to be some other way to get over this. Bake something. Knit a hat. Just not trolling the banks. All you're going to get is wet."

I looked between Gretchen and Tomás, one who didn't care if what I did made sense, and one who did. Which one was the better friend? The answer was: neither. They were both good friends, but neither of them wielded the power over me that Karen did. I didn't need to follow either one. I would listen to them, then I would make up my own mind.

Gretchen closed our locker and looked away. "I'll catch you guys after practice," she mumbled. "Stay inside."

Stay inside. Stay safe. Don't try to do this or that. Don't reach for something you don't understand; don't try to retrieve what you lost.

I couldn't stand the idea of being more isolated than I already was. It made me want to leap and bound like wildlife. It made me want to break free.

∽

I had every intention of sticking with track practice through the end, then going home like I was supposed to, but that changed when I got out onto the field and saw how little daylight I had left. If I were going to explore today, I had to do it now.

I went up to Ranger Dave, who had a whistle around his neck and was writing something on a clipboard. He was wearing a thin windbreaker against the rain and shorts, not sweats. I should probably mention that, even though I hated myself for noticing it (he was my coach after all), his thighs were impressively solid and lean. There was an inverted "v" shape just above the knee where tendon met muscle. They were the legs of a serious runner.

Thighs or no thighs, Ranger Dave was a good guy and I hated lying to him but I was about to do it. "Hey, coach," I said, trying to appear breezy.

"Ready to go?" he said without looking up. "Why don't you warm up with an easy fifteen hundred? Then we'll do some wind sprints."

"Sure. A bunch of us wanted to know if we could do our fifteen hundred cross-country. We're getting tired of the track."

He smiled to himself. "I hope not. The season's just started."

I said nothing, just stood there waiting.

He sighed. "In a group?"

"Just Allison and Nolan and me." I pointed to where Nolan Chapman and Allison Lehman and some other fast twitch guys were still lunging and pushing against walls.

"All right. To the Tiki Hut and back. Okay? Stay together and whatever you do, don't stop for cocktails." I half
laughed with him. I'd seen what people looked like after
Tiki Hut Scorpion Bowls. They were usually puky. And
handcuffed if they tried to get into a car, thanks to Sheriff
McGarry.

"Got it. No cocktails," I said.

I jogged around the track, trying to make it look as though
I was headed toward Nolan Chapman and Allison Lehman
while I was actually running past them. When I was on the
opposite corner of the field, and Ranger Dave had his head
down studying a stopwatch, I ducked out the gate and onto
the Santiam River Road. And then I sprinted like a buck till
I was out of sight.

At least there was no danger of my getting tanked, because the Tiki Hut was not my destination.

Much as I hated to admit it, Gretchen was right about one
thing: I had no method. I was just stumbling along, hoping
I'd trip over something. So today I thought I'd try a different
approach. I began at the mouth of the river, where the blue-
white water churned and frothed before becoming the placid
oily surface of Detroit Lake. I'd found Karen upstream from
here, so I didn't expect to find anything. I just wanted to
have something to chart, proof of where I'd been. *See,
Gretchen? I've covered this. I can be systematic.*

Combing this part of the river was much slower than
above the inn, because this stretch had houses along it. Not

many, but enough that I didn't feel comfortable tramping through backyards. Sometimes I did it anyway. *I'll know what I'm looking for when I find it.* Maybe there was something of Karen's still ensnared, circling the current. Did she have shoes on when I pulled her out of the river? A hair bow? I couldn't remember. I just wanted something that the river had kept, something that left a trace. *Here. Karen was here.* But it wasn't just traces of Karen I was looking for — it had to be Karen combined with something else, a larger footprint, a casually dropped match. Something that would ignite the whole town and light the way to what really happened.

Alas, as the sky went from gray to indigo, I came to the sad conclusion that the river was still harboring its secrets. I found traces of pollution but nothing to light the way. Just empty cold medicine wrappers, one Happy Meal toy, a smashed and rusted can of Bud Light, and something that looked like a purple plastic zucchini.

I was between yards, in a section of land that was huge and weepy with old growth, when I heard thrashing in the bushes and caught sight of something large and brown that looked like Tomás' poncho.

"How did you find me?" I called.

No response from the bushes. Just more thrashing.

A cold current of fear shot through me. "Tomás?" I tried again.

That brought about a noise. Not speech. This was low and rumbly and sent tremors to the ground under my feet. Definitely not Tomás. Tomás didn't growl.

I froze. Out from tall grass and horsetail ferns stepped the biggest hellhound I had ever seen in my life. It was the color of mud and its head was the size of a watermelon. It curled its lips back in a snarl.

Some of my friends love big dogs, always saying what was there to be afraid of, that most of them were giant cupcakes. I was definitely not a big-dog person. Thor was as large a dog as I'd been around, and this beast had a hundred pounds on Thor easily. Second, Sheriff McGarry once showed me this impressive red and puckery scar on her calf from where a rottweiler had dug into her when she was investigating a domestic disturbance.

There was nothing domestic about this canine. No collar, no leash, just a length of rope looped around its neck, its end trailing off into the bushes. He was head-to-toe mud and worse. Red showed through brown. He had multiple scratches and his ears looked like Shredded Wheat. Mud seemed to be the only thing holding this beast together.

And the smell. Hoo-wee! It was as though he'd been rolling in, then eating, a week-old skunk carcass.

We faced off, the beast snarling but not leaping at me, and me definitely not doing what my entire body told me to do, which was turn around and run.

"Hello?" I called hesitantly. "Will someone please come get your dog?"

No response from anyone other than the animal, who snarled louder.

I had no idea how this was going to turn out. I did know that if this creature managed to knock me down I'd have to cover my face and hope that the bites wouldn't disfigure me. Those were some wicked-looking jaws. And there were ropes of something gelatinous hanging from its snout. I couldn't tell if it was foam or really thick drool.

And that was when I started counting its ribs. One two three four five . . . the outlines of them were all clearly visible beneath the hide. When was the last time this animal had eaten? Six seven eight . . .

"Are you hungry?" I ventured.

No reaction. Hackles were still standing straight up on its back. He still didn't move.

I rifled through the pockets in my shorts and found a cell phone and a banana-flavored PowerBar. Slowly, I drew it out and peeled back the wrapper.

I held it out to him. "Dinner?"

The beast stared at me. Grrrrr . . .

"Treats?" I tried again.

No response, but at least he still didn't lunge. Come on, Ronnie. Mom would know how to make this sound appealing. "Yummy yummy treat. Definitely doesn't taste like banana-flavored asbestos."

The dog bellowed and I took one giant step back.

"Look, I'm sorry," I said, waving the PowerBar around. "I've just never had a dog, okay? And this move out here. It's been really hard. I lost a lot and there's no one I can talk to about it."

I wasn't paying attention to the dog now. Out here in the middle of nowhere, I felt like I could complain and no one would hear me. So I gave myself permission to have a good whine. "I miss midnight movies," I began. "I miss Starbucks. I miss all-ages shows at the Crystal Ballroom. And guidance counselors. Good ones. Man, don't get me started on that. You know, I actually tried to go to one of the counselors at Hoodoo High to talk about which safety college I should apply to? I thought, maybe St. Olaf. That one in Minnesota? They have a great choir. And do you know what that guidance counselor said? She said, 'We just got some information about St. Olaf last week and we threw it away. We never send anyone to St. Olaf. What about U of O?' Can you imagine? Me at U of O? She meant well, I guess. She was thinking about the track program. But come on. U of O is huge. I mean: what about class size? What about liberal arts?"

In front of me, the animal was silent. Was it my imagination or had it cocked its head? It was almost as though it was studying me.

"But that's not the worst of it," I continued. "You know what the worst of it is?"

I paused for a reaction but none came.

"I sometimes forget that Karen isn't coming back. I'll be still for a second and think: she'll come by later and we'll share a cream cheese brownie and go exploring. And then I remember that she's gone and it just hammers me, because when Karen was around I didn't feel so alone."

I sank to my knees. I had lost the face-off. The dog could pounce now, savage me, scar me for life, and I didn't care. I probably wouldn't even feel a thing. I put my head in my hands. "Come on now, boy," I whispered. "Bring the rain."

I sat there, empty, and waited for an attack.

It didn't come. After a while, I heard a snuffling sound and looked up. The empty wrapper on the ground told me the dog had woofed the PowerBar, and was now nosing me in the head and arms as though I were a tasty treat, and I let him. I jerked my head up and looked in his eyes. Close up, they were soft and brown, almost gentle. Then, while I was trying to figure out what to do next, his tongue darted out and drenched my whole face in a disgusting, slobbery kiss.

"Gross! I even had my mouth open." I wiped the saliva off my face with the back of my sleeve. I sniffed the air. In close range, the smell was even worse.

I stood up slowly and took in the length of him. His hackles were down and he was wagging his rump where a tail should have been. We were comrades now — all because he knew either from my words or my smell that I was the one creature in the Santiam National Forest who was probably as miserable as he was.

What now? Hesitantly, I grasped the rope around his neck and yanked the other end, which was still somewhere in the horsetail ferns. With one good tug it slithered free. It was short, ending in something big and dirty and rusted that looked like a railroad spike. I glanced from the hellhound, along the short rope, to the spike, and back. I thought I could piece together what had happened. Someone had kept this beast on a short chain and he'd broken free with sheer muscle power. Maybe I could find the owner and the owner would put him right back. On a short chain. Without food.

No. That was absolutely the wrong thing to do. But what was the right thing? Ranger Dave would know. I took the cell out of my pocket, called him, and explained the situation. He growled. "Jesus, Ronnie. How could you do that? I turned around and you were gone but Allison and Nolan were still here. How was I going to explain this to your parents?"

"I know. I'm sorry."

I heard him breathe heavily into the mouthpiece. "All right. Come out to the road, I'll find you."

The animal and I galumphed along together, me keeping a loose grip on his rope. I knew that if he charged someone there was nothing I could do. But I held on anyway because I liked the illusion of control. He seemed to as well, first forging ahead and then looking back to make sure I was following. Come on, slowpoke.

When we got to the road, Ranger Dave was already there in his US Forest Service SUV. He opened the passenger door. "Get in," he said. His tone was terse. I encouraged the critter into the backseat and got into the front. I didn't say anything. I'd never seen Ranger Dave mad before, and it scared me.

"Call your dad right now," he said as he eased the car out onto the highway. "Tell them we're going to the vet. Tell them about the dog. Don't mention where you found it, okay? Just say it wandered onto the track."

I muttered a thanks and said something about making it up to him. His disappointment filled the car as much as the 150-pound dog in the backseat.

"Damn straight you will," he said. "You can't keep wandering off like that. It's dangerous."

"So I'm told," I said.

He wagged a finger at me. "Don't get smug, missy. We've got to find a way to curb your recklessness."

"What did you have in mind?" I asked.

"I don't know right now. But believe me. There will be consequences." He sniffed the air. "Pee-yew! Have you looked for dog tags?"

"No tags," I said quickly. This beast belonged to someone before, but that someone had forfeited him.

Ranger Dave just nodded and cracked the back window hoping to dissipate the stench, and the dog spent the ride with his disgusting snoot in the open air, looking mournful.

At the vet's office in Salem they took charge and knocked

the dog out with a short-acting anesthetic so they could stitch up his ears and clean out the deep cuts. While we waited, Ranger Dave paced the parking lot talking on his cell, presumably with the Humane Society or Animal Control. I didn't listen but figured he was trying to rig it so he could adopt the hound and let it convalesce at the ranger station.

At last the vet himself emerged, a guy with a gray moustache wearing scrubs with cartoon puppies and kittens on them. He was holding the dog on a leash. It was one of the funniest sights I'd ever seen because the beast was wearing some kind of inverted lampshade on his head and kept running into walls. Step, step, *bonk!* Step, step, *bonk!*

"Here you go, young lady," the vet said, handing me both the leash and a bag that said "Salem Veterinary Associates" on it. "Food dish. Canned food so she'll put on weight. We gave her her shots. You're really lucky. You've got yourself a fine girl under all that muck. Looks to be a purebred mastiff."

I stood there openmouthed, holding the leash in one hand and the bag in the other while *she* sat on my feet and swatted good-naturedly at me with her front paw.

"Ronnie," Ranger Dave said. "She wants you to pet her."

No no no. This was all wrong. *She* wasn't mine. I wasn't a dog person. I was especially not a mastiff person. A mastiff with ragged ears and, let's face it, a really foul smell. There didn't seem to be a centimeter on her hide that wasn't shaved, or stitched, or gross, or all three at the same time. I didn't want to pet her. I wanted her out of my life. I'd already done my part, hadn't I? I'd rescued her from starvation.

I turned to Ranger Dave. "This is just for the ride home, right? You'll take care of her, won't you?"

"Not me," he said, and smiled an impish smile. And I understood. I stared down into the dog's face — *her* face — and knew that I was looking at the big hairy snout of my consequences. Ranger Dave hadn't been on the phone with the Humane Society. He'd been on the phone with my parents who had decided it was a fine idea for me to have a pet.

My mood didn't improve on the car ride home, either, because the oaf wouldn't stay in the back seat. She would creep up on silent paws to where I was riding shotgun, and try to plunk herself into my lap. She seemed to think that if she was really slow and quiet, I wouldn't notice her. It didn't work for two reasons: 1) she wasn't dainty, and 2) that lampshade kept getting in the way. I pushed her back twice, furious each time. As far as I was concerned, she was just one more thing anchoring me to a life I didn't want.

By the third time I gave up trying to push her out of my lap. It was easier letting her have her way. I arrived at the inn cradling 150 pounds of muddy, stinky dog.

Mom and Dad were enjoying hot buttered rums on the front porch, safe and dry under the eaves with an outdoor heater pointed at their legs. Mom picked up a tray from the railing.

As soon as I opened the car door, the dog hopped out and careened up the front steps (walk walk *bonk*! Walk walk *bonk*!). Mom stood up and whipped the linen napkin off the tray. It was piled high, volcano-style, with grilled sausages and carmelized onions. The smell made me salivate worse than the dog, and I realized how hungry I was.

Then she plunked the tray on the ground, and I understood that, once again, the food wasn't for me.

"Now let's see. These have chicken, apple, and cumin, and those are andouille, and these are chorizo . . ."

It didn't matter. The dog put her head down and they were gone in one massive slurp. Then she looked up, belched, shook her head, and the slobber went winging all over the porch. I thought for sure that now Mom would be disgusted, mutter a few phrases about health code violations, and make us find the dog some other home. But she just laughed. It was more than a laugh, it was actually a cackle. I couldn't remember the last time I'd heard Mom cackle. It took ten years from her lined face.

"Are you sure this one's okay?" Dad said to Ranger Dave. "Couldn't we start with something smaller?"

"This is exactly the right one," he said, and Dad didn't question him further. Ranger Dave knew his critters.

Mom sniffed the air. "Too bad about the aroma," she said.

"Do we have to wait until the stitches come out until we can bathe her?"

But then a funny thing happened. It was like in horror movies when halfway through the film you stop sympathizing with the heroine and start sympathizing with the serial killer. When Mom made that comment about her pungent bouquet, this beast with the brindled schnoz of death stopped being *a* beast, and became *my* beast. And I couldn't have anyone dissing *my* beast.

"She's not so bad," I said. "She smells just like a petunia."

With that, Dad opened the front door and Petunia herself trotted right in, proprietarily, as though she'd lived here forever.

15

Petunia wasn't the only consequence of my recklessness. I was also grounded from using the family car for two weeks, which meant Dad had to drop off Tomás and me at school, then pick us up after practice, like in kindergarten.

That first afternoon of chauffeurage, Tomás and I were camped out in front of the gym while the fast twitch kids were still stacking hurtles. They gave me all kinds of grief when Dad pulled up in his SUV with Petunia painting the back window in slobber. "Look, Ronnie. Your *daddy's* here," Nolan Chapman said.

"Hi, Tomás," Allison Lehman said with a sly little wave.

Tomás acknowledged her with a thrust of his chin, and continued his slow lurch to the car.

"This sucks," I hissed to him. "How come my stock has gone down and yours has gone up?"

Tomás paused with his fingers wrapped around the door handle. His brow was a "v" shape of concentration. Then after what seemed a half hour, he turned to where Nolan was, and slowly, deliberately, flipped him off.

"That better?" he said as he crammed himself into the shotgun seat.

"Yes," I said. And surprisingly, it was.

Even before I sat down Petunia was crawling into my lap and thrusting her snoot into my face. I managed to get an arm up to block her but her lampshade scratched it. When I pulled away to inspect the damage she zoomed in for a full-face slurp.

"What does Ranger Dave say about dog breath?"

"Live with it," Dad barked.

When we walked through the front door of the inn, I hung up my dripping rain jacket and dropped Petunia's leash. Dad stopped me with an "Uh-uh-uh, Veronica. What do you think you're doing?"

"Washing my hands then prepping?" It's what I did most afternoons. I figured after I'd been so grievously busted I would be chopping cilantro for the rest of my life.

Dad leaned over and picked up Petunia's leash, giving the end to me. "First you need to walk your dog. Do you have your mace?" Now this was more like the old Dad. He knew, even without my telling him, that I had no idea where my mace was. I'd lost track of it as soon as Sheriff McGarry gave it to me.

I didn't need to say anything before Dad was on me again. "How 'bout your phone?"

That was something I had a response for. "It's in my backpack."

"Pull it out, then."

I undid the front zipper and foraged inside. It was usually right here, underneath the lip balm and PowerBar. Except that it wasn't. I dumped it upside down on a lowboy. Three tampons, a handful of change covered in a mysterious brown dust (old Oreos?), a pair of sunglasses, but nothing else spilled out.

"Try the main pocket," Dad suggested. So I upended that, too. Chem textbook; *Literature for You*, Second Edition; *¡Hola!*, Fifth Edition; three subject folders and corresponding spiral notebooks; a folded schedule of track meets, a pair of really smelly ankle socks, and that was it.

"Huh," I said. "I could've sworn I put it in there this morning."

"Well, you're not going outside until I see your cell fully charged and switched on."

"It's all right, Mr. Severance. I've got mine." Tomás was standing behind me. Then he thrust his Motorola out for Dad to inspect. That made it twice that day he had come to my rescue. And while I didn't like feeling helpless, it was kind of cool having someone back me up. I could see why the guys on the basketball team loved him. It wasn't just for his height.

But Dad wasn't done with his interrogation. "I suppose you have her mace, too."

"Right here," Tomás said, popping the cap and tossing it to me.

"Flashlight?"

"Check," Tomás said.

Dad softened. "Thanks, Tomás. Good thing *one* of you is organized."

Then he shot me a last stern, disapproving glance before retreating to the Astro Lounge.

After reloading my backpack, we went out the sun porch and down the back steps, Petunia on one side of me, Tomás on the other. I thought: *This is insane. Dad might as well have handed Tomás to me on a leash, too.*

The river was higher than it was yesterday, and it made me anxious. I knew it was just runoff and that's what happened in the spring, but to me it meant that I was losing ground and *la llorona* was gaining it.

"I wonder what happened to my cell," I mused aloud.

"You missing anything else?" Tomás spoke up. He was so graceful and quiet, for a minute I had forgotten that he was there with me.

"You mean like my iPod? And Dad can't find some of his antidepressants." I suddenly understood what he was talking about. He wasn't accusing me of being impractical. "Come on. You heard Dad: I'm disorganized. I just misplaced that stuff."

"Even your dad's drugs?"

That stopped me. Could he be right? Was someone ripping us off?

"What about your purse?" Tomás went on. "Do you still have cash in your wallet?"

"I don't know." It wasn't something I checked a lot, which might seem strange, but there wasn't anything in Hoodoo to buy.

Tomás frowned. "We should go back. We should go back right now and check."

"I already have a father, thanks," I snapped. I was lucky to be out — on or off a leash — considering all the trouble I was in. And I didn't want Tomás telling me how to spend what little freedom I still had.

I hadn't even gone two strides before I was sorry. Had not the man come through for me twice today already? And no, that didn't entitle him to run my life, but that was what siblings were about. Or so I was told. We might drive each other crazy but we couldn't walk away. Besides: I had no trouble dealing with Esperanza waking me up at 2:00 in the morning, and she hadn't even flipped anybody off for me.

I was about to apologize but he did it first. "That was way out of line," he said. "We're all a little freaked. I just thought..."

He stared at his shoes. Something was dammed up inside him, like it was the day Karen had prodded him to ask me something that he never got around to. "You just thought what?"

"I don't know. I guess I thought we were safe."

I nodded, I thought so, too, and the feeling wasn't even that strong with me, because I still saw the inn for what it wasn't, namely the city. But Tomás was different. He needed to be here, cocooned by his family and mine. And I wondered what he was escaping.

"What do you need to be safe from?" I said.

Tomás rubbed his wrist, the one with the impressive scar. Safe from whatever had given him that. In a lot of ways he was like *la llorona*, I thought, careful about giving up secrets. But if I had to guess what he was talking about, it wasn't just that his dad had gotten drunk and knocked him around. He was talking about rage and death, the darkness that stumbled past my bedroom window every night in the old house. Whereas I had the luxury of watching it progress from warmth and safety, Tomás had to live with it. That darkness was probably what he thought he'd outrun, and then it had overtaken Karen.

"It's all right," I said. "I don't need to know."

I looked at the sky, which was now the deep purple of boysenberries. Once again I was dead-ended. "I suppose we should get back."

I jerked on Petunia's leash and started back toward the inn, trying to avoid the stinging nettles. I heard Tomás' voice over my shoulder. "There's something I want to ask you."

I turned around. I wondered what he was going to say, but had a feeling it had nothing to do with his scar. It was as though a little trickle of freedom was coming from him, and it was my job as his near-sister to encourage it into a steady current.

"Shoot," I said.

There was another long pause. That was okay. I could wait. "Do you know anyone who would go out with me?"

I almost had to ask him to repeat himself, because that wasn't the question I'd been expecting. I didn't realize I'd been expecting anything, but at that moment I knew that I had — I'd even rehearsed what I would tell him.

While I was puzzling over this, I lost my footing and fell face forward, right into something hard and scratchy. I tried to pull myself together, but the bushes weren't letting me go. Petunia helped me by sitting on my feet and swatting me with her front paw. *Get up.* I managed to get myself disentangled and into a sitting position, feeling my throbbing forehead. A thunderegg was forming above my right eye.

"Are you all right?" Tomás said, and extended his hand to help me up. I didn't take it, because I noticed something hidden in the tall grass. Something shining, like a diamond, where everything shiny should have been snuffed by the darkening sky.

"Hand me the light." I took it and inched my way over to the object on all fours. It was just more junk — an empty cigarette package. I picked it up tentatively as if it was a dead bird. Why did I need a closer look at this? I saw junk all the time.

Then I uncrumpled it and looked at the label.

Jakarta.

Reading the letters made me feel glacial, like the moment before all your fingers and toes go black from frostbite — that moment when you still have feeling but you know you have to get out of the cold.

"Isn't that Keith's brand?" Tomás asked.

"It doesn't mean anything," I said. "He's always bank-combing for junk for his mom's art projects. I see him around here all the time." And that part was true. The smokes probably had nothing to do with Karen's murder. All they really proved was that Keith had been through here.

So why was something whispering to me that this wasn't right?

Look, Ronnie, just look.

All those months following Karen around. She had trained

144

me to spot the unusual. And so, even though my first reaction was to deny I'd even seen this, something deeper told me different.

"Ronnie . . ."

"I don't want to hear it."

I got to my feet. I shone the flashlight all around the ground and along the bank. There were no shoes, no hairbows — not even any Happy Meal toys. Tomás looked around, too. Five feet upstream there was a tall cedar and lots of brambles. No way anyone could maneuver around it. That must be what happened: Keith was out here looking for stuff for his mom, had a smoke, turned around, and went home. It was the rainy season. He could leave his butts out here without torching acreage.

"I can't do this anymore today," I said. I should have said, I don't *want* to do this. I'd been looking too hard, trying to make sense of a senseless death, and I was circling like an eddy.

I started walking back to the inn.

"Hold up," Tomás said, took the flashlight from me, and shone it in my eyes. The bright light made stars explode in front of me, strong as mace.

"You're bleeding," he said, and brushed something off my temple.

I ran my tongue over my upper lip. It tasted like rain and something else — something liquid and tangy.

"Does it hurt?" he asked, drawing away his hand. His fingers were red.

Yes, I almost said. Because when he drew the flashlight away from my face, I first saw fireworks, then when they cleared up, the outline of his face. It was so strong and his eyelashes so thick that for a moment it didn't matter to me that he wasn't hip or was never without his baseball cap.

This wasn't right. I couldn't be attracted to him. He was almost like a brother. Besides, what about Keith? I fingered the cigarette pack in my pocket. That didn't prove anything. He was probably still my rock-star hero.

Still, looking at Tomás' profile in the boysenberry sky, I couldn't help thinking about how I'd never had him and now I had to give him up, the one who flipped someone off for me, and the pain of that alone was enough to make my face throb.

"Ronnie? Does it hurt?"

I closed my eyes and listened to the river. I didn't know what I was feeling, but I knew I deserved the pain.

"No," I said. And I tried to believe it.

16

Mom wanted to take me to the ER to check out the lump on my forehead and see if I was concussed or needed stitches. Tomás thought it was a good idea, too. I didn't want to drive an hour to the closest hospital then wait another two for some resident to send me home with an Advil and a pat on the head. I touched the Jakarta wrapper in my pocket. I was so tired. I just wanted to crawl under strata of quilts and dog hair and sleep.

Luckily Ranger Dave was in the Astro Lounge. I might not have been a bear cub and so was outside his area of expertise, but his CPR was current and we all trusted him to referee. He came upstairs, poked me a bit, asked if I'd lost consciousness, and when I said no, told Mom and Dad not to worry, that head wounds always bled a lot, which neither of my parents found particularly comforting.

"You might not be a forehead model for a while but you'll be okay," Ranger Dave said to me with a wink.

Dad forced a laugh and Mom poured herself a glass of merlot.

The next day I woke up tender and swollen. I thought about skipping school and going back to the patch of briars where I'd found the Jakartas, but I couldn't make myself, because thinking about it broke me in two.

So for the next three days I stayed on the track and bleachers, chopped herbs, and read to Esperanza. I hoped that if I kept to where I was supposed to be, eventually I wouldn't feel so jagged. It didn't work.

And then it was Saturday.

ॐ

The first real hint I got that Gretchen's party would be so crashingly bad was the beer Jell-O.

It went something like this: Dad drove Tomás and me to Gretchen's that night. He wouldn't let us walk even though and it was less than a mile and Tomás was a hulking menace of a guy with evil-looking facial hair. "It's not that I don't trust you — I don't trust other drivers. It's a dark road," Dad said, overenunciating as though he were delivering a closing argument to a hostile jury.

When we pulled into Gretchen's drive, Dad questioned me. "Got your mace?"

"Check." It was clipped to my purse.

"How 'bout your cell?"

"Check." My new phone was on a special pouch on my belt. We'd finally agreed that my first one had been ripped off (not lost) and Dad had another one overnighted to us. I kind of liked accessorizing with tech. It made me feel important, like Batman.

"Call when you need picking up, all right? And Ronnie: Try not to go outside. Another thing: If you have to make out with someone, make out with someone large. Like Tomás here."

"Dad!"

Tomás slunk down in his seat. He was balancing a tray of appetizers on his lap and they threatened to topple.

"All right, then," Dad said. "Have fun!" Tomás and I got out of the car, Tomás carrying the blue corn tortilla chips and guasacaca, a dip with layers of guacamole, corn, black beans, repeat. Like a bean dip volcano only with cilantro, which, if you asked me, Mom was now using way too much of.

I thought Tomás and I were done with Dad's particular brand of humiliation, but as he was backing out, he rolled down the driver's side window and lobbed a fresh insult at us.

"You two look so cute together!"

At that point I didn't see how the evening could get worse.

∞

Gretchen's house was the beige rambler with bright magenta trim. It was the one funky place in the neighborhood. No amount of pressure washing and beauty bark could disguise the fact that the porch was slouching. The foundation was rotting out from under them. And no surprise — the ground underneath all of us was sludgy mush. The only thing holding most places upright was ice, but that was melting. You got the feeling that, when the thaw came, Gretchen's house and a dozen more like it would just run off into the sea.

We walked up the front drive, our ears assaulted by the throbbing bass of the White Stripes. We knocked on Gretchen's front door but there was no answer, so we let ourselves in.

I went down the hall past the art deco prints of harlequins ("Cinzano '74!") to her bedroom. The door was closed so I rapped on it. "Gretch? Tomás and I are here. We'll set up. Take your time."

The rattling noise came not from her bedroom but from the bathroom next to it. There was a clatter like something falling to the floor, then a hushed "shit" from a voice a lot lower than Gretchen's. Then Gretchen's voice shushing him and giggling.

"Gretchen?" I called. "Are you okay in there?"

"Yeah!" she said loudly. "Be right out!"

I stood at the closed bathroom door for a few more minutes, trying to figure out who was in there with her. Who deserved my funky friend? I couldn't picture her and her purple-tipped hair with a baseball cap guy.

At last I gave up eavesdropping and went to help Tomás set up. She'd come out sooner or later. I'd examine her new man then.

The dining room was a small space between the kitchen and the back patio. The table was glass and chrome. Not chichi, but clean. In the center was a clear bowl with royal blue marbles in the bottom, like a fake aquarium. It was very Zen-like. All that was missing was an orchid or bamboo plant — something spindly and contemplative.

Tomás had removed the centerpiece and was spreading a cloth over the tabletop. I went into the kitchen and pulled the plastic wrap off the chips and dip. As I did, I saw the chore list tacked to the fridge. It read:

> *Gretchen. I want you to:*
> *— Make an olive rosemary loaf*
> *— Clean your bathroom*
> *— Feed the cat.*

Already half in party mode, I decided: something has to be done about this. There were many things in my life that

I had no control over, but for one night I could fix Gretchen's list. So I tore it up. Then I found Gretchen's mother's Post-it notes and created a new list:

> Gretchen, I want you to:
> — Make the beer Jell-O
> — Vacuum the cat
> — Pick your nose thoroughly
> (not the half-assed job you usually do.
> I mean it. Get parts of your cerebellum.)

I put it on the fridge and forgot about it because there were dirty dishes in the sink and I was determined to help.

I should probably mention that Gretchen had these little rebellions. To begin with, her room was out of bounds from her Mom's nitpicking. The dirty clothes on her floor had more layers than the guasacaca. Second, she never strayed from the list *ever.* If there was a heap of dirty dishes in the sink, but no item on the list that said "wash dishes," Gretchen would let them pile up and attract flies, which was apparently what had happened tonight. There were pans crusty with spaghetti sauce and salad dressing and caked-on flour. Scouring them was going to give me upper-body definition.

I was still washing Gretchen's dishes when the bathroom door finally opened, and Keith came staggering down the hallway.

Even though I hadn't had anything to eat or drink yet, my stomach felt like I'd just slammed a volcano of bean dip and chased it with cheap tequila. Keith? In the bathroom with Gretchen? Giggling? Maybe it was . . . no. There was no way I could make that into something innocent. I had to face it: they had hooked up.

I leaned over the sink and bit my lip. They didn't even like each other. How could they do this? *To me?* Gretchen knew how I felt. Even *Keith* knew how I felt, and neither of them cared.

Keith turned up the music and started slam-dancing around the living room. I tried to look at him without his catching me at it. He was wearing his army jacket and reeked of clove cigarettes. *Just how bad are you?* I thought.

He mowed into Tomás only half on accident. Tomás pushed him off with extra oomph.

"Sorry, *Dumbass*," Keith said.

"That's Tom-*ás*," Tomás said.

I turned my back to them and focused on a piece of crusty something that wouldn't come off this cast-iron skillet. *Keep moving*, I told myself. *As long as you keep moving it isn't real.*

Tap tap tap. Keith was trying to get my attention.

"Hey," I said. I was feeling much colder toward him than I had an hour ago.

He belched in my face. "You know what? You're really pretty."

That was all he said. He walked off and opened the back door to Gretchen's deck. Then, with Tomás and me both watching, he unzipped his pants and peed into Gretchen's mom's juniper bushes.

He zipped up, came back in, took a blue corn chip from the platter, and dipped it in the guasacaca. "Dude," Tomás said. "At least wash your hands first."

What was going on? Was he into me after all? Then what was he doing with Gretchen in the bathroom just now? I was so busy wondering that I didn't notice Gretchen herself had come into the kitchen, retrieved the newly cleaned cast-iron pan from where it was drying on a rack, and was heating water over the stove. Her hands were busy, almost flailing. One of them was cooking and the other one scratching everywhere — her arms, her legs, but mostly that spot on her scalp that she'd been digging at all week.

I won't ask what they were doing in the bathroom. It's her business. Let it go.

"What's up, Gretch?"

She opened the fridge, twisted off the cap of a Moose Drool Ale, and took a deep swig. "Gotta stick to the list," she said. And she dumped the rest of her beer into the pan with the water and a packet of unflavored gelatin. "The Corning-Ware's in the left-hand cupboard," she said.

Holy cow. She was really going to make beer Jell-O. This was silly, but at least it was something I could get behind. "The kind with the little blue flowers?"

Hah. A little rebellion, potluck-style.

I found the casserole dish she was talking about and put it on the counter next to the stove. The cooking ale lent the place the heavy smell of a brewery. When she judged the concoction ready, she poured it into the Corningware pan. "Shouldn't it have some fruit in it? Maybe grated carrots?"

"Good idea," she said and went to the fruit bowl sitting on the counter. She removed a banana from a bunch.

"Want me to cut that up?"

"Nope," she said. And plopped the whole thing in, peel and all. "Now we can just let it chill awhile and voilá. Where's Montgomery?"

Montgomery was her cat. He had limited outdoor privileges. They usually let him out around sunset to catch garter snakes and moles. He was probably patrolling now. Unless I missed my guess, he was about to get vacuumed.

Gretchen went off calling "Monty!" and scratching her temple.

There was another tap on my shoulder. I turned around and there was Keith again. "I think I'm gonna kiss you," he said, and then went off to Gretchen's stereo to change the tunes from hip-hop to punk.

Tomás handed me a blue corn tortilla chip. "Did you hear that?" I asked.

Tomás nodded.

"Do you think he was serious?"

"Maybe," he said. "But don't get your hopes up. That guy's an asshole."

And you're a buzzkill, I thought.

People had started arriving by this time. Casey Burns came with a case of Bud. Allison Lehman and Nolan Chapman arrived together, but she dropped him as soon as Tomás said a timid "hi" to her.

And that was the way it went for the first two hours. People came in, I pointed to the beer and reloaded the guasacaca tray when it emptied. If anyone wanted to smoke I made them do it outside. There was no way we would be able to hide from Gretch's mom that we'd had a party, but that didn't mean we had to trash the place.

Finally, two hours later I was circulating a garbage bag for empties when I got another *tap tap tap* on the shoulder. Keith turned me around and gave me a giant spicy kiss. There was no preliminary, no tentative peck on the lips. *You into this? I'm into this.* No, this wasn't about give and take. He ground himself against me, scratchy and confident. It felt more like ownership, as though he was showing to everyone in the room, me included, that I was his.

Then he pulled away from me, his hands still cupping my face. "I could make you feel *so* good," he whispered loudly. And even though a tiny part of me knew it was wrong, I was oh-so ready to let him try.

I didn't get a chance because there was Tomás, prying

him off me, his eyes fiery with rage. He slammed Keith into the fridge, forehead first. It was so violent, I kept thinking: *This can't be him. He would never . . . he doesn't move this fast.*

Keith got up, his forehead bleeding, and tackled Tomás, running him backward into the dining room table. Blue corn chips went flying everywhere. "Asshole!" Keith dealt him one good punch in the eye. There was a crunching sound that didn't come from tortilla chips. Tomás kicked against him hard and the two went flying back through the kitchen.

I heard myself shriek, "Do something! Do something!" But I didn't know who I was talking to. People gathered around the two of them, but no one tried to pull them apart. Some were even tugging on cans of Budweiser, like they were watching a Mariners game. This was ridiculous. I tried to grab Tomás from the back but when he cocked his arm I got an elbow in the nose. Man, that stung. I let go and waited for my eyes to stop watering before jumping in again.

I was getting ready to make another run at pulling them apart when there was a *tap tap tap* on my shoulder, and there was Allison Lehman, hopping on one foot. "I know this is a bad time, but some of us have to pee."

"Why are you telling me?" I spat.

"The only bathroom's been locked for an hour," she said. That got my attention. I skirted the fight and ran down the hall. "Is anyone in there?" I called as I pounded on the door.

No answer. I tried the lock; it rattled but didn't give. I shouldered the wood but it stayed firm.

And I didn't need *la llorona* to tell me something was wrong — something worse than a brawl. From the dining room came the sound of shattered glass and heavy bodies slammed against the floor.

Allison was still behind me, openly holding her crotch. "I don't care what you have to do — get Tomás out of the scrum," I told her. It might just be a problem with the lock, in which case Tomás could fix it in a jiff.

In the meantime I sprinted outside to find another way in. This was no time to wait and see what happened. I could feel my heart pounding, *ba-doom ba-doom ba-doom*, as though a starting pistol had just gone off with a loud *crack!*

I didn't know what was happening behind that door. I only knew that this time I had to be fast.

From far away came the sound of the river. *Run, Ronnie, run!*

17

I count the number of windows until I find the frosted pane of Gretchen's bathroom. It's closed tight. I tug on its runner to see if I can knock it into sliding open. I even brace myself with one shoe against the frame — but even though I pull until my fingernails crack and bleed, it won't budge. I'll have to smash it.

I look around the flowerbed for something to lob against it. God damn it, why don't these people have gnomes? There's nothing. Then I notice the black sealant around the glass is rotting. I give it a good tug and it whips off in long black strings. The window slides down the wall and shatters on the beauty bark. Shards fly up and embed themselves in my pant legs. I feel sharp stings up and down my thighs and know that a few have broken through.

No time to worry about that. I hoist myself up onto the sill, which is high and skinny, and do a front roll over it, landing in the shower with a hard blow to my back that knocks the wind out of me. The plastic rubber ducky curtain comes down on top of me, wrapping me like a shroud.

Wincing, I dig myself out and look around. Gretchen is unconscious on the floor. There is vomit everywhere. The smell is sharp — like puke and worse. Gretchen's jeans are wet around the crotch.

She is so still, I flash back to Karen's body on the riverbank. Oh no. Not again. *I can't do this,* I think. But I know I have to. I offer up a silent prayer to someone to intercede with the gods of CPR on my behalf. *Karen? Help me out here?* Then I roll Gretchen over on her side, fishing around her vomity mouth. I don't pull out anything because she's already thrown everything up. It's in her hair and on the tile.

"Gretchen!" I yell, pounding her back. "Gretchen, wake up!"

Her eyes don't open.

Then I notice the mirror. Someone has taken it off the wall and spread it over the sink. There's a dollar bill unfurling on it and white residue.

Whoosh! Terror runs through me. She and Keith weren't in here having sex — they were in doing hard drugs. I am so over my head, I'm drowning.

Shit. I put two fingers to her neck and get a pulse like a jackrabbit's. *Ba-doom. Ba-doom. BADOOMBADOOMBA-DOOMBADOOM.* I'm glad her heart's still beating but really really wish it were slower and more regular.

She comes around with a jerk.

"Get them off me!" she yells, digging at her arms, violently scratching as though she is being devoured alive. I hold her right arm out, the one that's bothering her. There are big red furrows where she's scratched them raw, and they're oozing yellow smelly pus. Something reddish black flares out under the skin, like a spider web. I can't tell if it's blood or poison.

At that moment there's a crash and the door explodes half off its hinges. Tomás comes barreling in. "Jesus," he says, taking in the scene. Three kids try to follow him in but he holds them back, blocking their view. I hear a murmur, then Tomás responds forcefully: "Use the bushes. We're busy in here."

Gretchen stops scratching her arm and moves up to the spot on her temple I'd seen her digging at before. I pull back her bangs. What I see is like a scene from a horror show. Gretchen has scratched herself so deeply that her skull is showing, and she's still digging at it.

I pull her hand away and pin it to her side. "Stop! Let me go!" she screams hysterically. "The spiders! They're still there! They're crawling all over my body! Somebody take them off!" She smacks at me, trying to get me away from her so she can scratch herself raw. We wrestle until we're both covered in vomit.

"Help me!" I squeal. "Hold her down!"

Tomás takes over my spot and, pulling my cell phone from its handy spot on my belt, I finally get a clue and call 911. I know I am getting a lot of people in trouble but I don't care. Gretchen's in a bad way and I don't know how else to help her.

Let me tell you, nothing clears out a party faster than sirens. Within ten minutes we hear them; within eleven everyone has peeled out and the entire night sky is flashing red. A troop of burly uniformed medics, none of whom looks older than me, comes through the door.

"What seems to be the problem?" the first one says. He can't be more than twelve. I don't have a ton of faith in their ability to deal with what we're dealing with.

A second guy takes Tomás' place holding down Gretchen. "What did she take?" a third hurls at me.

All I can do is look dumb.

"Meth," Tomás says. I look up, he's leaning against the half-broken door. How does he know for sure? White stuff on a mirror could be anything.

But one look at him tells me: *He knows*. He's talking from experience. I don't know how, but he knows exactly what meth is and what it does to a person.

Then I notice the rest of him, like how the skin around his right eye is puffy, as though sprouting something, and how he's clutching his chest in pain.

"Do these guys need to take a look at you, too?" I say.

"Focus, Ronnie," he grunts, as though even speaking is an effort. "*I'll* live."

And those words scare me more than anything I've seen so far tonight. Damn it, not Gretchen. I already had someone I love die this week. Statistically, shouldn't two be impossible? But I know it doesn't work like that. There's no limitation on how much a person has to bear.

The medic kneeling over Gretchen is saying something into a walkie-talkie, having a conversation in code with a doctor on the other end.

They fire more questions at me like how old is she, how much does she weigh, and is she allergic to any medication. I answer the best I can. Sixteen. Not much. No.

"Get them off me!" Gretchen is yelling. It takes two burly guys whose thighs are bigger than my waist to hold her down.

The one who's been questioning us asks, "How much did she take? How did she take it?"

I point at the mirror and the unfurled dollar bill.

"We don't know how much," Tomás says.

"Can you find out?"

"No," Tomás says.

I take in Tomás' swelling eye. "He chased off her source."

He looks Tomás up and down. He finally says "Dude!" in a way that sounds as though he would like nothing better than to smack down some drug dealer, but since Tomás has beaten him to it, the medic can only bask in admiration. Then he turns to me and says, "I recognize you. You were the girl who discovered the last body."

"No, she isn't," says the one who is holding Gretchen down while the other squirts some kind of thick liquid out of a syringe. "*That* girl was Veronica Severance and as a non-family member she can't ride with us in the ambulance. Try again."

The Dude turns to me, his face now somber and efficient. "What is your relation to the victim?"

I say slowly: "I'm her sister. And this guy is her brother."

Tomás can only nod in agreement. He is shaking now, leaning heavily on the door. Something inside him has cracked.

"What are you doing to her?" I say as the one guy jabs a needle into Gretchen's arm so hard blood drips out.

"This is nothing, ma'am. Just a mild sedative. It'll calm her down for the ride. Hopefully they'll clean her up at Salem General."

But Gretchen is still writhing and screaming. She's out of her head in pain. I don't know how much more I can watch, and yet I know I won't leave unless they make me. I have to keep her together by willpower alone. "How long til it takes effect?" I ask.

"A few minutes," he says. "Now let's go."

I look behind me. There are another two burly kids wheeling a gurney toward us down the short hall. It's time for me to get out of the way and let people who know better do their work — people who maybe don't have a lot of years behind them, but at least are comfortable around needles and aren't flummoxed by hallucinations or vomit or rotting flesh.

I walk over to where Tomás is standing and wrap an arm around his back, knowing that he'll probably kick me away, this big macho hero vigilante. "Come on. You can lean on me."

Instead of shrugging me off, he brings his other arm and lays it over my shoulder, then gently leans against me.

The two of us together follow the gurney outside, step, hobble, step, hobble. Tomás is gripping his side and he's so heavy. But I don't mind. Moving slowly like this brings my heart back to normal speed. And just as we climb into the ambulance, I can feel that racing *whoosh!* slow down to a strong and steady beat. Which is just as well. I can't keep up this panic that makes me feel as though I were sprinting even when I'm standing still. If I'm going to help the people I have left, I have to pace myself.

18

At Salem General they abandoned the idea of Tomás and me as Gretchen's family and wouldn't let us go with her into the treatment room while she was being "stabilized."

Sensing I was about to pitch a hissy fit, one of the medics took me aside and said, "She'll live. But starting tomorrow she's in for a world of hurt."

While they were speeding Gretchen through triage and into an empty bed, some burly guy nurse with a Semper Fi tattoo and scruffy hair caught sight of Tomás wheezing, clutching his ribs, and sprouting a massive black eye. He said, "Man, let's get you looked at, too."

He tried protesting but Semper Fi Guy led him back to the triage nurse talking gently the whole while, as though he were dealing with some lumbering and nervous animal.

I was left alone in the waiting room with a saltwater aquarium, a woman in full burka with a screaming baby, and reruns of *Friends* playing on the wall-mounted TVs. I'd left my purse at Gretchen's so only had my cell strapped to my belt. I tried calling Dad but they wouldn't let me because it interfered with medical equipment, so they booted me out to the parking lot.

When I finally reached him, he was alert — almost combat-ready. I looked at my watch. No wonder. It was way past our curfew. "What happened to you, Ronnie? Your mother's tearing her hair out. We heard the sirens but by the time I got to Gretchen's everyone was gone. I got your purse, by the way." I listened to the tone of his voice, trying to gauge his mood, and how much I should disclose. I was afraid if I told him everything it might push him into some dark abyss.

"How much anti-anxiety meds you on, Dad?"

There was a pause on the other end as he braced himself. "Enough," he finally said. So I came clean.

I told him about the beer Jell-O. I told him about the mirror and the hard drugs. I told him that I should've seen the signs but didn't because I thought she had allergies and kept baker's hours. And I should've known that she was stealing my stuff because how many other people had access to my locker and nightstand, where it had all gone missing?

He kept quiet through the whole thing. And when I was done, I held my breath and waited for him to react. Would he yell? Cry? I just dumped on him a whole lot of civilization, and he moved us to Hoodoo to escape civilization.

"Dad?" I prompted.

"You did the right thing," he said, sounding like his old, competent self. And the idea that after all these months he might be able to back me up again made me want to cry more than anything that had happened so far tonight. I had my back to the ER window. I leaned on it and slowly dripped down, til I was squatting in a mushy heap on the ground.

"Ronnie? Are you okay?"

"I'm fine, Dad. It's just been so *hard.*"

"I know, honey," he said. "Hang tight. We'll pick up Joanne and be there in an hour." Joanne was Gretchen's mom.

I didn't have a Kleenex so wiped my nose on my sleeve, leaving a snail trail. It was gross, but at least the tide of my mood was ebbing.

"Dad?"

"Yes, honey?"

"Come quick. I'm tired."

I heard him breathing on the other end. "I love you, sweetheart," he said, and hung up.

I looked back inside through the waiting room window.

Marine Nurse came out of a set of double doors and called something I couldn't hear.

I went back into the hospital and walked up to him. He was wearing a nameplate that said *Curtis.*

"You're the girlfriend, right?" he said.

"Probably," I said.

He nodded. "Come on back with me. You're being paged."

I followed him through a set of double doors along a linoleum-floored hallway past a set of semi-private bays. In one of them, Gretchen was stretched out on a bed with tubes up her nose and in her arms. Her eyes were closed and her hands were still. Three people in scrubs were working efficiently but not hurriedly around her. I paused on the threshold. I heard one of them say "blood work" and "pregnancy" and "HIV." They looked up, saw me, and a woman in royal blue scrubs firmly closed the curtain around Gretchen's bed, blocking her from my sight.

We turned a corner and he led me into another bay. Tomás was lying under a white blanket, a thin gown with tiny blue flowers tied loosely around his neck.

"Hey, baby!" he called casually, in a smooth un-Tomás-like tone. He held out his hand, beckoning me closer. I took it and he scooped me to him, planting a smooch on me that made Petunia's kisses seem dainty and refined. And I let him. Because kissing him felt really good. It wasn't like kissing Keith — he didn't make me shake with excitement and panic. No, this was different — comfortable but exhilarating at the same time. His breath was cool but had a tart taste to it, as though he'd been gargling with iced limes.

He made an "Mmmm . . ." noise.

I pulled away, but just slightly. He looked at me through those long lashes, and his gaze was soft, like a puppy dog's. Something had smoothed the punctuation right off his face.

"You're on something, aren't you?" I whispered.

"Yummy yummy Percocet," he breathed.

"Among other things," said the nurse behind me. He was looking at X-rays on a screen. I saw the ghosts of ribs, a neck, and very long finger bones.

"Kiss me again. You taste like bean dip," Tomás said, tugging on my arm.

I looked at Marine Nurse. "Did he try to make out with you, too?"

He snorted. "Yeah, but I'm not cheap like you are. I told him I don't do that on the first date." He smiled indulgently. I was really happy that we'd landed with him. He oozed casual confidence, as though he'd already been through combat and nothing else fazed him.

"Come over here and check this out!" he said. "Looks like your prince fractured a rib and his collarbone. The thumb, too. Now that we can splint," he said, and chortled like he'd made some kind of dirty joke.

"Wait, a collarbone? He plays basketball. What is that going to do to his playoff chances?"

170

Curtis didn't say anything. He just shook his head. Basketball season was over.

"It's all right, Ronnie. I don't care too much about winning. I'll play next year. Besides, most of the college scouts have already seen me. I'll get a scholarship."

"What a trouper," Curtis said, clucking with approval. "I hope you're worth it, babe."

"Worth what? The broken collarbone? That wasn't for me," I said.

"Yes it was, *corazón*," Tomás said.

"No it wasn't. He got into it with Gretchen's pusher."

"Which one is Gretchen?" Curtis said.

"She's my other girlfriend," Tomás said.

The medic smirked. "You hound."

"Not that kind of girlfriend. Not like *gordita* here."

"I am not your *gordita*."

I didn't mind humoring him. I liked seeing this side of Tomás, the side that had moves. I didn't know if he was really interested in me, or if he just felt so good it didn't matter who he charmed. I had to draw the line at *gordita*, though, because it meant *little fatso*.

"Whatever you say, *mi cielo*," Tomás said, gave my hand a squeeze, then puckered his lips, waiting for a kiss.

Looking at him, so unclammed up, gave me an idea. "Excuse me," I said to the nurse. "May I please have a moment with my prince here?"

The nurse snorted and backed out of the bay. "Sure

171

thing, *gordita*," he snickered, and ran the curtain closed behind us.

As soon he was gone Tomás pulled me to him again. I kissed him for a bit and tried to tell myself it didn't mean anything. Chances were, tomorrow when he woke up I'd have to release him back into the wild. I understood that his shyness built a fort around him that would take some heavy artillery to breach, and I didn't know if I could do that. But for the moment I let us both think we belonged together.

When we came up for air, I whispered in his ear, "What did your dad do that was so heinous?"

"He had a meth lab," he said. And reached under my shirt to my waist. He ran his fingers across my bare stomach. They were cool and feathery.

"Meth? Is that how you knew what Gretchen was on?"

Tomás made the "Mmmm" noise again, and I took it to mean yes.

"How long have you known?"

"Since forever," he said.

He kissed me again and then smiled this evil guy/seductive smile, like Sting. Who knew this boy had moves? "Come to papa," he whispered, tangling his fingers in the curls at the nape of my neck.

There was a crack sound of a curtain being pulled back. "Son, I love you as though you were my own, but you'd better not be trying to cop a feel."

I looked behind me. Dad was there with Gloria Inez and two other guys I'd never seen before. They were clean and their hair was slicked back, and they wore badges like leashes around their necks.

"Oh, hey, Mr. Severance. It's okay. We're engaged," Tomás said.

"He's on pain meds."

"She's the love of my life."

Gloria Inez bounded ahead and grabbed her son's hand. "Ay, gordito, que paso?" Coming from her the word gordito didn't sound like an insult. It was gentle, like being covered in a warm quilt.

"May we borrow Veronica for a moment?" Dad asked Tomás.

The tilde went back to Tomás' forehead. "Okay. But only if you give her right back." Then he cracked himself up so hard he spat saliva everywhere. And his laughter was so infectious I laughed, too.

It was a hard night. Down the hall Gretchen was fighting something that was devouring her alive. Just thinking about it made me feel cold and puky, but here, in this room with Tomás, I was wrapped in warmth and citrus and fingers tracing butterfly shapes across my skin.

I walked out into the hallway still tittering, but sobered up pretty fast. Who were these guys with Dad? Police of some kind.

"Veronica, I believe you know Agents Sadler and Freeman of the DEA," Dad said.

Agent Sadler acknowledged me with a nod. Then he reached into a jacket pocket and read something on a cell phone. And that was what did it. Just a tilt of the head a certain way and I knew him. True, his hair wasn't mussed and there was no Tiger Balm on his lips, but there was no mistaking him now. There was no mistaking either of them.

"Good Brad?"

19

Good Brad couldn't help a chuckle. "I told you you were too patronizing," he said to his partner, Agent Freeman.

Evil Brad crossed his arms. "It's not my job to flirt with teenage girls."

Dad cleared his throat. "I would like to remind you gentlemen that I'm standing right here. And feeling very litigious."

I looked between the Brads and tried to picture them as I knew them. It was hard. Without the lip balm and ski jackets they looked like they were born to law enforcement.

"How long have you known about this?" I asked my father.

"It was my idea," he said. "I thought Patchworks might make a good staging area."

"Listen," Agent Sadler said, "we need your account of the incident. Is there some place we could talk?"

We wound up in a staff break room, surrounded by vending machines that sold Red Vines and SunChips and packages of crackers with Spreadable Cheez Paste. We sat down at the fake wood table. I dusted off the remainders of Doritos from the surface while Good Brad bought us Diet Cokes. Evil Brad sat there looking intimidating.

I popped the tab on my soda and swallowed deep. It was cooler than mountain runoff.

I set the can down on the table. And with a quick look around, to make sure that no one else was here, I whispered: "This is about meth, isn't it?"

Evil Brad threw up his hands. "Finally! The kid gets it."

"It's not her fault," Dad said. "We wanted to keep her out of it, remember?"

Good Brad took over. "We've been trying to shut them down for months. But if we're going to shut them down, first we have to find them. And they've camouflaged themselves pretty good. There's no trail, no nothing. All we know is they're parked out in the wilderness somewhere."

I flashed on a memory. That day on the riverbanks, when I refused to follow Karen across, and the squaring of her shoulders. She was going to go farther than she was used to.

What if she didn't just go once? What if she wandered off, say, every time she thought no one was looking? What if someone else was watching her, waiting for her to get close?

"You think Karen found it," I said.

Jesus, I thought, and bit my lip. *And I let her go. I practically dared her. Her death was my fault.*

I felt as though I were running and something huge and dark and faster than Alberto Salazar had overtaken me. I'd gotten through this difficult night just by finding the next step, the locked door, the bathroom window, holding Gretchen's arms down while she tried to claw herself. But now nothing I did was going to be clear.

"This is my fault," Dad said. "I moved us to Hoodoo. I thought I could get away. But as the agents here can tell you, I just landed us right in the middle of drug land. These guys practically have their own frigging cartel."

It was so easy for me to stay *stop guilting yourself* to someone else. But I couldn't rid myself of my guilt. All I could do was push it down hard into my stomach. For now that had to be enough.

"When you're ready, Ronnie," Good Brad said. "Just tell me what happened. We can't bring Karen back from the dead. But we can catch the ones who killed her."

"We'll go home," Dad conceded, as though he were surrendering. "Home to Portland. I'll call Catlin Gable School and see if you can finish the year out there."

"But what about the finding the lab? What about the cartel?"

Evil Brad spoke up. "We can take it from here. You tell us what you saw, Gretchen will give her account in the morning. That's probably enough to prosecute at least some of the parties involved."

Some of the parties. That had a hollow sound. Did I care? They were offering me what I wanted. We could go home. All I had to do was give them a name, then I would get everything back: the coffee shops, the boutiques, the clubs, the midnight movies . . . I could be me again, this whole year washed away as though it had never happened.

But could I really go back to the way I was before? No. Not yet. Somewhere underneath everything, all the things I thought I loved, even beneath the guilt and frustration, was a core that I felt but didn't yet understand. It was important to me to figure out what that was.

I closed my eyes and tried to think. Instead I heard running water, and beneath that, snatches of songs running through my brain. *Can you see the real me?*

Then I flashed on something odd, and it wasn't what I thought it would be. It had nothing to do with Karen or Tomás or *la llorona*. It had to do with the end of the movie *Quadrophenia*, when the kid stands up on the seat of his scooter and rides it off the cliff. I suddenly had to know: does he go with it? Or does he chicken out at the last moment and decide to live his life?

I wondered if Agents Sadler and Freeman could scare me up a DVD even at this hour of the night. I could watch the movie in the break room over and over so I could see if the figure on the cliff was a person, or the shadow of one. But that was not the way to get my answer.

There was only one way to solve the end of *Quadrophenia*. "Could I please see Gretchen now?"

Evil Brad pursed his lips in frustration, but in the end had to defer to my father the attorney.

"Of course, honey," Dad said, and he led the way out the door and back down the linoleum hallway.

∽

Gretchen was asleep, her arms still. The overhead lights were low but not off. There was no one in scrubs bustling around her. The only sign that she hadn't been forgotten by the medical staff completely was the steady *blip blip blip* from a machine to the right of her. Her arm, the one that had been leaking stinky pus, was tightly and thickly bandaged, mummy style. They'd pulled back her hair so we could see another thick bandage over her temple. Her good arm was hooked up to an IV.

Blip blip blip. Slow and steady, like a long-distance runner's — not the crazy BADOOMBADOOMBADOOM of the bathroom floor. Whatever the doctors had done had worked. She was stabilized — at least for now.

Gretchen's mom, Joanne Kinyon, was sitting next to her

bed. She was shivering in a rayon dress in which bloodred suns set behind black palm trees. There was a plastic lei around her neck. She was a tall and stern-looking woman. Not the kind you'd expect to be waitressing in a Polynesian restaurant.

She might have made a great office manager in another life, but there were few offices in Hoodoo, so she had to settle for managing Gretchen.

She looked up when we came in. He face was unnaturally smooth and broad, like a giant cherry soaked in rum. "How's our girl doing?" Dad asked, pulling up a chair.

"Oh, fine," Mrs. Kinyon said, when we could all see she wasn't fine. "The doctors cleaned out her arm pretty well and she's on antibiotics. Now we just have to wait and see."

"Wait and see about what?" I asked.

Dad hushed me with a look.

But Mrs. Kinyon replied to me anyway. "If she gets to keep it." The expression on her face didn't change. She looked competent and sure of herself, but she had begun silently to cry.

"Keep what? Her arm?" I asked, horrified and more shrieky than was appropriate.

Dad patted her on the back. "Apparently Gretchen's been at this for awhile, Veronica. There was gangrene."

Then Mrs. Kinyon seemed to notice me, really notice me, and deliberately didn't ask the question I knew she wanted to ask: if you two were such good friends, how come she's lying here and you're not?

I thought of all the defenses I could offer. Gretchen kept me out of it. I wasn't exempt because she ripped off my stuff to pay for her habit. But what it really came down to was that I was stupid, and there was no excuse for that.

Mrs. Kinyon wiped her face with her fingers and I offered her a paper towel. She thanked me and there was no blame in her words, just fatigue, probably realizing there was enough blame for all of us — including Gretchen herself.

"Four thousand dollars!" Mrs. Kinyon said. "That's how much it's going to cost to get her into Riverside. I don't have that kind of money, Paul. Where am I going to get it? She won't finish out the school year, and even if she goes there's no guarantee. The social worker said even with Riverside there's a ninety percent chance of relapse."

Riverside must have been a treatment facility.

She dabbed at her eyes some more. "I've been sitting here thinking about my options. And I've been thinking about kicking her out of the house. Can you imagine? My own child? I mean, what kind of parent am I? She's all I've got."

I wanted to reach out to her and say it will be okay, but I didn't, because I didn't know if it would. If what all of us wanted counted for anything, Gretchen would get to keep her arm and go back to school, clean and whole and scared straight.

"Joanne," Dad said softly, his voice dim and soothing as the lights in Gretchen's room. "Take the opening. We'll help with the expense. We'll find a way."

And at that moment, even though he was burned out, I loved my father more than ever. And all because of the we. *We'll* help out. *We'll* find a way. He was trying to help patch together someone who wasn't even his. And there, I realized, was something I could latch on to, a quality more true and solid than an army jacket and a pair of heavy black boots.

I slowly backed away. I didn't need to see any more. Not tonight. I had my answer.

I still didn't know what had happened between Gretchen and Keith in the bathroom. All I knew was that Gretchen was here in the hospital and Keith was not. Had he given her a stronger dose than he gave himself? Or had he just watched her ingest poison while he sat back and chugged beer?

Either way, I now knew the end of *Quadrophenia*: there were two people on that scooter, not just one. Keith had stood Gretchen on the seat in front of him, maybe whispering things like: *it'll be fun*, or even *I know how to make you feel good*. Then at the last minute he pushed her off while he rolled out of the way. He was the coward standing safe at the top while Gretchen plunged into wreckage.

I found the Brads leaning against a counter of a nurse's station, sipping Diet Cokes. Good Brad looked hopeful and pulled me out of earshot of anyone in scrubs.

"I didn't really see anything," I said.

"That's all right," Evil Brad said. "Just tell me what you did see. We'll get Gretchen's testimony when she comes around."

I hated him, standing on that cliff, watching from a safe distance. So I stole up behind him . . .

"They were in the bathroom. Two of them together. When they came out Gretchen was acting all strange."

"Who, Ronnie? Who was in the bathroom with her?" Good Brad said.

I saw him from the back in his Eisenhower jacket. He didn't notice me. With one hard kick, I toppled him over the side, too.

"Keith Spady," I said.

And there it was, the core of me. It had changed, but it was one thing I was now sure of.

I didn't need any more rock-star heroes.

Hey. Whacha doin?

Cooking.

Karen is in her yard, busily putting together something messy. I've finished my Saturday run and stop to look. Karen always has something worth looking at.

It is fall and raining. Of course. We haven't had a first frost yet but it's coming. There's a bite in the air.

I look over Karen's shoulder. She's arranging heaps of mud on a plank, putting a tall blossom in the center of each. They look like fat purple wands.

Wow. Great presentation. Mom would be impressed.

Thanks.

There's a pile of these delicate purple blossoms wilting next to her. I pick one up and sniff. It gives off no scent.

What do you call these?

Blue lupine, she says. *They're really rare this late in the season.*

A-ha, my little delicate mountain flower, I say, nudging her. She smiles at me. We both know that *delicate is an insult to this girl, up to her elbows in mud, squatting out here in the rain because the project she's working on isn't yet the way she wants it. She is solid and complex, like a thunderegg.*

I look again at the bloom in my hand. Where did you find these?

She doesn't answer, just goes back to rearranging the mud in buttes, one high-altitude flower marking each peak.

Karen? I say. Where did you find these?

She lifts the plank and offers me her creations. Have a brownie, she says.

20

It was a long dark drive back to Hoodoo. Dad was silent. Tomás was stretched out in the backseat, his arm in a sling to keep the collarbone steady. Occasionally he would stir and Gloria would hush him down again with songs about frogs and baby ducks.

Up in the shotgun seat I watched the timber run past and thought about landscapes. I thought about the landscape of Tomás' face, the scratchiness of his chin, the smoothness of his cheek, the softness of his eyes. I thought of how good it felt kissing him, the feeling of his fingers tracing butterflies on my skin. He was more than just a good guy — he was a discovery. He was *my* discovery. I felt like, after a long journey, I had finally found the Pacific Ocean.

Then I thought about the landscape of Gretchen's mind, and the plans she'd had to be a graphic artist and how the whole thing was flooded by her addiction. I liked to think there was something of the original Gretchen underneath, a ghost town of personality from before. My guess was that was long gone, and she'd now have to build something entirely new.

And then I thought of the landscape around me, the one out there in the dark, the one that whispered and wailed and gorged itself on secrets.

Finally, I thought about blue lupine.

When we made it home and Tomás was safely tucked in, I went down the hall to my room, where Esperanza and Petunia were stretched out asleep. Petunia lifted her head when I came in. "Shhh . . . *ya gordita,*" I said softly, and watched her eyes slowly close. Then, as quietly as I could, I turned on my computer and Googled *lupine.*

Karen was right — it shouldn't be here at all. It was a meadow plant, and there weren't a ton of meadows along the Santiam. Plus it was March now, February when they had turned up in Karen's last mud pies, the beginnings of the fat purple wands I'd seen last fall. Lupine was only supposed to bloom in May and June, which led me to believe that Karen must've found a spot with a lot of sun.

I stared at the screen, memorizing the blossoms, the mandala shape of the leaves, until I was confident I would be able to identify them if I found them again.

But where to start looking? How did a person even begin to look for a meadow?

It turns out I knew that, too.

Careful not to wake Esperanza, I slipped on my running gear, clipped my phone to the waistband of my sweatpants, and wound my way downstairs. Petunia trotted behind me, refusing to be hushed a second time. That was all right. After all, Petunia had to come from somewhere, too. Somewhere she was kept on a short chain with no ID. I didn't know that she could help me find my way, but I didn't mind having her along.

I flicked on the light in the sunroom and reached for my raincoat. There, in the pocket, was the crushed packet of Jakartas I'd found that evening with Tomás, when I knew something was wrong but still didn't want to believe it. Keith had defeated me that day. I'd turned back because of him. No more. It was up to me to finish. *Don't worry, Karen, you can rest now. I'll bring us home.*

Outside it was cold and raining, the sky still dark. Holding the flashlight in one hand, I picked my way upstream for what I hoped was one final time, my heart bounding in my chest, my legs so jittery they were ready to sprint.

Race day had begun.

21

Even though it wasn't yet dawn, and the raindrops were so huge they made the whole landscape look unfamiliar and drowned, I had no trouble picking my way back to the spot where I'd found Keith's cigarette pack. It was as though the memory was stored in my legs. I shone the flashlight on the briar barricade. It was just as bad as before — a solid wall of brambles there was no skirting around — and they hung so far over into the water that you'd practically need waders to get around them.

I didn't hesitate. I hopped in.

Yee-ouch! The current was so cold it was painful. This

wasn't water: this was liquid ice, and if I didn't get out of it soon it was going to kill and preserve me, like some woolly mammoth. *Runnerus domesticus. She tried but didn't get very far.*

I willed my legs to move. One foot upstream, then another. I was amazed I could even keep my footing. When I finally rounded the bushes the current became gentle. I was in an eddy. I shone the light to the shore beyond. There, tied to the trunk of a cedar, was a rowboat.

I dragged myself to the shore with Petunia dog-paddling behind. I fiddled with the ropes but it took awhile. My hands were shaking with cold or fear or probably both. But finally I was able to pull it free and hop in. Petunia launched herself in after me, practically upsetting the whole craft, but after a few anxious moments we got our balance and I began rowing.

It felt good to work my muscles. I was able to replace my fear with something else. Movement. Reason. Maybe what I was doing wasn't so dangerous. After all, if the rowboat was on this side, then hopefully no one was opposite? I could just case the joint, row back, and lead Brad straight to it. No one even had to know I was there.

The sky was turning purple by the time Petunia and I reached the opposite bank and I pulled the boat onto a rocky shore, tying it to a metal hoop that had been placed there just for that purpose.

I looked up. It was light enough that I could make out the shapes of trees. Lots of them. There wouldn't be enough sunlight for lupine to grow here. I shone my flashlight on the ground. *Splunk.* The rain was coming down so thick it was like being pelted with dodge balls. But still, they hadn't completely washed away the prints in the mud, huge prints from someone's square-toed boots. They led straight up a narrow path that seemed to disappear in the clouds. That was one difference on this side of the river: this side was a lot steeper.

"This is it," I said to Petunia, and the two of us began picking our way along.

There were places where there was nothing of the path but a mudslide, and others where we had to scramble over boulders. But I was guided by Petunia, who was not only surprisingly agile, but seemed to be familiar with the route. She trotted ahead of me and then looked back to make sure I was still there. Part mastiff; part mountain goat.

After the sun came up and I didn't need the flashlight anymore, I began smelling something, something industrial like bleach or ammonia. What needed cleaning way out here?

And the higher we got, the lighter the rain and the thinner the trees, until the rain stopped and there was an anemic Northwest sun. We were at the edge of a clearing with a straight view to the top of a snowcapped peak. Don't ask me which one. There were tons of peaks around here. This one was probably too short even to merit a name.

Ahead of me, there was still snow on the ground, large fields of stuff so thick in spots it was blue. But in between were patches of brown, and from the brown poked up very small, very fragile-looking plants with mandala-shaped leaves. I went up to one and leaned over. There, in its middle, was the stubby beginning of a purple bud.

I heard a click and froze where I was crouched. Then there was familiar voice saying, "Here you are, Rocky! I was wondering where you'd run off to!"

I slowly turned my head. There, sitting right under the timberline, so subtle I hadn't even seen it, was a mobile home painted in brown and green camouflage. And sitting on its back steps was Keith Spady. My faithful hound Petunia was delicately crawling into his lap.

Had he seen me? I didn't know. I was out in the open, only a few feet from the timberline, trapped in plain sight. But he hadn't looked up. I stayed in that crouch with my heart hammering my chest until I was satisfied he didn't know I was there. Then, slowly, I scuttled crablike to the cover of the trees. I'd have to leave Petunia. Maybe she'd find her way back without me. But maybe, just maybe, while she was in Keith's lap, she could buy me the time I needed to get away.

"Where've you been, girl, huh?" Keith puckered his lips

and made kissy noises at her. "Looks like someone's been taking care of you."

I was three steps away from the cover of the trees.

I watched as Keith found her collar and reached around.

Oh no. I knew exactly what he would find. Only two more steps.

He had found her tags. *Petunia. Veronica Severance. 555–3636.*

His head shot up and he looked around. His eyes were big red plums, and his nose had a butterfly bandage over it. He looked like a ghoul. A big, bloody, broken-nosed ghoul.

He was looking around for me but it didn't matter. I was in the tree cover now, I could easily slip away.

And that was the exact moment my cell phone rang.

Shit shit shit. Oh no. I plucked it out of my belt and lobbed it into the bushes away from me, where it sat, still ringing. But I was too late. I had looked at Keith and he had locked my gaze.

I turned around and ran. *The river. I've got to make it to the river.* It was downhill so I had gravity working for me. But so did he. I sprang like a deer and was so close I could almost hear the rushing water, when he tackled me from behind, sending the both of us sprawling down in an avalanche of rocks and pebbles. The two of us came to a stop when we collided with the base of a Douglas fir. I kicked and scratched but he rammed himself up against me, pinning my arms to either side of my head. I tried to head-butt him but he jerked his face out of my reach. It was no good. He had me.

We stood there heaving, trying to catch our breath. I had to get away from this guy, but not now. He was just too strong. I would have to try something else. I willed my heart to slow down. This wasn't going to be a short sprint after all — this was going to be about endurance. Fortunately over the past few months, I'd gotten good at enduring.

"I've decided to take you up on your offer to make me feel good."

He didn't buy it. He smiled his ghoulish smile that had nothing appealing about it at all.

"A bit late for that, Ronnie, don't you think?"

22

He followed me up the trail to the timberline. Petunia was there, sprawled underneath the Winnebago. Traitor. Where had she been when I was careening down the hill for my life? Some guard dog she turned out to be.

Keith opened the back door to the mobile home and thrust me in ahead of him, announcing, "Hey, guys, look what I found!"

Two people looked up and glared. I recognized both of them. One was wearing a Hawaiian shirt and had gray hair pulled into a ponytail. That was Keith's stepdad and Mrs. Kinyon's boss, Phil LaMarr. The second guy was Robbie Markle, another kid from school. He was a skate punk, kind of like Keith, but without Keith's savoir faire. He was short and round through the middle. I always thought of him as Barney Rubble to Keith's Fred Flintstone.

Phil scowled. "Well well well," he said. "What are we supposed to do with this?"

Something unsaid passed between Keith and Phil. They were going to kill me, they were just debating how. My mind raced with terror. BADOOMBADOOMBADOOM-BADOOM. Then I thought I heard Karen's voice running through my head.

Look, Ronnie, just look.

Man, this place was disgusting. Aside from the noxious smell there was the orange shag carpet caked with bits of things, cigarette butts, moldy bits of old meals, and used condoms. Somebody had been having sex in this vile place, and unfortunately I had a good idea who. *Gretchen, what have you done?*

Every surface was cluttered. There were filthy pans piled in the sink and on countertops, layers of week-old mac and cheese still in evidence. The only surface that wasn't completely covered with gunk was a kitchen counter where a hot plate was plugged in. On top of it was a beaker, giving off heat and that awful industrial smell that had polluted the whole Santiam National Forest.

"I thought we might keep her around for a while first," Keith said, stroking my arm.

"Keith," Phil rasped. "This isn't a good idea. This one has people who care about her. They'll come looking."

"Gretchen has people who care about her, too. So did Karen," I said.

Phil didn't have any reply for that.

Look, Ronnie, just look. There are spaces between them. Silences that can be widened.

The door was behind me, the only person between it and me was Keith, and Keith's eyes were poofy slits, so his vision couldn't be good. If I could get him to loosen his grip, I might be able to make it off this mountain.

I stepped down hard on Keith's foot. He let go of me, briefly. "You bitch!" he yelled, and grabbed me before I'd made it two paces to the door.

"Get her!" Robbie yelled.

Phil opened a drawer in the kitchenette and pulled out a length of rubber tubing.

Keith slammed me headfirst into a table. I saw stars.

"Keep her arm steady!" There were two of them keeping me bent over the table now. Keith over my back and Robbie holding my arm out, tying something tight above the elbow. The circulation below my shoulder stopped. This was how Gretchen got gangrene.

They flipped me over, Keith pressing his whole body against me, even rubbing his crotch against mine. "Shh . . . ," he kept saying, as if that would make a difference. He was going to help kill me and it excited him. I had no idea a person could be so sick.

"This is the best way to go. You'll see."

I arched my back and screamed in raw animal pain.

Boom! The back door slammed open and there she was. I'd gotten so used to her as a cupcake, I'd forgotten that there was a menacing side to her as well, and this was it. Her lips were curled back into a growl, revealing her pointy canine teeth. She still had on the goofy lampshade but behind it her hackles were high and pointy as porcupine quills.

As we stayed there immobile, my elbow brushed against something bulky on my side. My Bat Utility Belt. The cell was gone, but it was equipped with something else. I just needed a little more wiggle room.

"Petunia!" I screeched. And that did it. She charged for Keith's calf, sinking her teeth into it and worrying it like a rawhide bone. Keith screamed and let go of me. At the same moment, I brought out the mace and sprayed it on whoever was near. Phil got the most of it, but Robbie got some as well.

I didn't wait. I ran.

Behind me, I heard Keith yell to Robbie, "Get the gun!"

I didn't even try to get my footing on the way down the hill. Branches and rocks pulled at me and tripped me. I had to get to the rowboat. My life depended on it. I was spry as a mule deer.

Behind me, I heard the pounding of four paws. Petunia

had gotten free and was catching up. *Atta girl!* I thought. Then there was a loud *bang!* that stopped me cold.

I whipped my head around in time to see Petunia jump up and sideways in an unnatural way. *Kay-yay! Kay-yay!* I went a few steps to get her but stopped because right behind her was Keith holding a pistol which he was now pointing at me.

Bang! Something whizzed past my head. I ducked and kept going. I had to get away. I was in earshot of the river. *Run, Ronnie, run!* it cried.

I heard shouts coming from all around me. "Over here! This way!"

Then I was at the shore, pulling back the cedar branches. The boat was still there, tied to a stake where I'd left it. I fumbled with the rope, muttering under my breath. *Comeoncomeoncomeon* . . . but it was no use. My fingers were too wet and I'd tied the knot too tight.

There was crashing through the bushes behind me. He was getting close. So I gave up on the ropes and sprinted downstream. Another option gone.

Run, Ronnie, run! the river urged.

There was another *bang!* and the whole world exploded.

Some people say that when you get shot you don't feel it right away. But I did. Something that definitely was not brambles had hit my leg hard and sent waves of pain through my entire body. I cried out and went down fast. I gripped my calf, which was all bloody and felt like it was on fire. But just as bad as the pain was the fear that this wasn't yet the worst of it — that the worst was chasing me, bloody-eyed, through the undergrowth.

And then the river stopped urging me to run. Maybe I'd lost too much blood and was going into shock, but I thought I could see water splashing up against the banks, and it took the shape of a woman who dissolved into spray then re-formed with each splash. A woman who wasn't crying but was smiling at me, her arms open wide, ready to embrace me. *Come, Veronica. It will be easy. You won't feel a thing.* And at that moment, surrendering to that embrace didn't seem like such a bad option, especially if I didn't go alone.

I now knew what I had to do. Maybe the river would take me, too, and maybe it wouldn't. I didn't know. All I knew was that it had its own kind of justice, and that it needed me to extend its reach.

I pulled myself up behind the Douglas fir. The river was behind me, eating at the banks.

And here came Keith running half-blind, carrying a pistol. I didn't move; didn't breathe. Everything depended on his not seeing me until it was too late.

He drew nearer. Ten yards. Five. Two. One. I let him get one footfall ahead of me, grabbed him from behind, and pulled us backward into the current.

Whoosh! La llorona did her part, sweeping us away as

soon as we hit the cold. I let go of Keith and tried to get my head above water. I came up gasping, my lungs making an unnatural sucking sound. And then I went under again. I was above water long enough to see that log floating ahead with all the jagged branches sticking out. There was a scratch and I heard something break, I wasn't sure if it was part of me or a branch.

I tried to grab hold but the log just rolled with me underneath. I pushed free and tried to surface. I opened my mouth and felt muddy water fill my lungs. I was drowning. But then at the last minute I was able to bob up. *Slam!* I impacted with something that wasn't moving, something slick. Even as I tried to get a handhold and claw my way up, my legs started to drift to the side. I felt myself slipping down, but with a last effort was able to get my upper body over the rock and stay there.

All around me *la llorona* smiled and leaped and reached out to me with watery hands.

I thought I heard someone calling my name. *Ronnie!*

I told the river to shut up. It had me already.

Ronnie!

There it was again.

I looked up. There was Tomás standing on the banks, more solid than water. He was wearing his brace but his arm was out of it, so it looked like he had a white scarf draped around his neck, a bad fashion statement.

"Take my hand!" He was grasping a tree branch and leaning out in the current.

"Your collarbone!" I called back.

"Just take it!" his voice was louder now, more shrieky and urgent. And with that, he let go and leaped in.

"Jesus!" I said. What an idiot. Didn't he know he could get himself killed like that? I had to get him.

We reached each other halfway between the shore and the boulder. He grabbed my hand and pulled me to him. The two of us rode the current, up and down and up again. When I went under, we both went under.

"This isn't working!" I yelled the next time we surfaced.

"I'm not letting you go!"

Then we stopped. Had he hit another rock? That couldn't be it because slowly we began to make progress toward the shore.

I felt someone haul me up and slap me down on the grass. I looked up. I saw everything through a veil of rain but they were all there, muddy and wet, a human chain that didn't break. *Red rover. Red rover. Send Ronnie on over.* There was Mom and Dad and Ranger Dave, Tiny, Sheriff McGarry, the Brads. And at the front, half submerged but still standing, his eyes darting with panic, was Mr. Armstrong.

One the bank, someone turned me on my side and whacked me on the back over and over again. I spat up what tasted like a gallon of muck.

"She's been shot. Stanch the bleeding. Call 911."

Mud and pebbles came trickling from my mouth.

"Other side," I said. "Look for the rowboat."

"It's going to be all right, Ronnie," I heard someone say. Then: "Get the damn ambulance!"

"Wait!" Evil Brad said, then leaned in close. "What did you say, Ronnie?"

I repeated myself. "Find the rowboat. Up to the timberline."

I saw a look pass between the Brads. "We're not going anywhere until the ambulance gets here," Good Brad said.

I shook my head: no no no. "It's a mobile home. They can just drive off."

Dad broke the stare-down. "We've got her! Go!"

The Brads sprinted upstream. "They shot Petunia," I tried to call after, but Tomás hushed me as his mom had hushed him last night. "*Ya, gordita*," he said, cradling my head in his lap. "*Ya ya ya.*"

I felt someone tie something off my leg just above my knee and there were pinpricks and stars all over — especially in front of my eyes. Off in the distance I thought I heard wailing. But it wasn't *la llorona* this time — it was sirens.

"Is that for me?"

"I hope so," Tomás said.

The sirens, instead of growing louder, grew fainter. I felt as though I were going under. Before I blacked out completely I saw something drift past us in the current — could have been a branch, could have been an arm. But it had to have been a branch because nobody moved to pull the arm out.

Mr. Armstrong watched it drift by.

Tomás just gripped me tighter.

I am sitting on the banks of the river, which is once again low and gentle. I am contemplating a smooth stone in my hand. It seems important but I can't remember how. What am I supposed to do? How do I cock my arm? Do I throw underhand, like a girl? Do I try to put topspin on it?

Across from me, Karen steps out of the woods, kicks her flip-flops off, and wades across in surefooted strides.

Wordlessly, she sits down next to me. I can't see her whole face. I only see her profile. I can feel something swell up, filling my throat like a thunderegg. This isn't right. She shouldn't be next to me. It's what I want, but it's not the way things are supposed to be.

She picks up a stone, cocks back her arm, and lets it fly. Skip. Skip. Skip. Plunk.

Now I remember. That's how it's done.

Why are you crying, Ronnie?

I feel her voice rather than hear it.

I failed you, I say.

How?

I was supposed to go with you, remember? That one day? You wanted to cross over but I wouldn't let you?

Ahhhh . . . she says, the gentlest sigh, caressing my ears like a breeze. You were a good friend.

You're just saying that because I gave you chocolate.

She reaches into the current, selects a flat, smooth stone and lets it fly. I did like the chocolate, she says. But I liked that you spent time with me, too. Some people used to get me confused with my brothers and sister. Not you.

No, I say. I never wanted you to be anyone else. You were special.

She nods. And that's why I came back. It's time to let me go now, Ronnie.

I know, I say. It's just so hard. I'm afraid I'll forget you.

You won't forget me. Look, you remembered how to skip a stone, didn't you?

That's different, I say.

No, she says. No different. I'm in your blood now. Like river water.

She gets up and starts forging her way back across.

Karen?

She stops.

If you want, I can go with you. I'm not afraid anymore.

She half turns to me. I know you're not, Ronnie. But you can't.

She takes another two steps, then stops. You will tell them, won't you?

Who?

Mom and Dad. Tell them it's okay. There's lots of territory to discover over here. It's really just one more frontier.

It is my turn to sigh. It makes a certain kind of sense, this dream-logic.

I'll tell them, I say.

Karen, satisfied, turns to me full on. I can see all of her and she isn't shining and glorious, she is just Karen and I miss her and I will never get her back. She smiles sadly, squares her shoulders, and waves goodbye. I count her steps like skips of a pebble. One . . . two . . . three. Nine steps to make it to the other side.

Nine steps and she is gone.

23

One . . . two . . . three . . . nine steps.

Nine steps down from the courthouse to the street. I've gotten good at judging distances, when I should use the crutches and when I should just hop. This time I choose the crutches and am able to step-swing those nine steps down without losing my balance and toppling forward into a Tri-Met bus.

I look up. The courthouse is one of the funkiest buildings in Portland, all geometric tile, as if a kid had built it from blocks. On its front is the second-largest bronze statue in the United States. Portlandia. She's huge, a goddess with wavy hair holding a trident in one hand, reaching down with the other to scoop boats out of the water with the other. From where we are, I can only see the bottom of one massive bronze hand.

Gretchen stands on one side of me, lighting a cigarette. It's a nasty, stinky vice, but it could be a lot worse. She takes a drag and I look at her profile. She's filled out a little, not much, but at least there's color in her cheeks. She's lopped off the purple fringe in her hair and now looks almost ordinary.

She has two arms. She's wearing short sleeves and the scar on her right elbow is *not* colored in. She usually likes to doodle on it, decorate it with ivy like a Victorian stencil, but Dad has threatened her with incarceration if she tries to make it look any less ghastly than it is.

"I think that went well," she says.

I turn around and look back inside. Dad is still in there, talking to his old cronies, even though now he's no longer one of them. He's a prosecutor now, and he's a nasty one. The jury's just been given their instructions. Phil LaMarr has been escorted somewhere far away from civilized people. When the jury comes back, I hope to hear the word *remanded*.

∽

We are back in our home in the city, Mom and Dad and Petunia and I. I'd forgotten how small our house was. The dog takes up half of it. She was my biggest worry that day on the river. I kept crying for her on the Life Flight helicopter all the way to Portland. Or so they say. I remember the tears,

I remember being frantic. Then I remember Dad, trying to calm me, saying, "Trust Ranger Dave to fix her." I remember thinking, "Oh, yeah," and passing out again.

The next thing I knew I was waking up in the hospital, Tomás asleep on the visitor's chair. I took a good long look at his profile. He wasn't wearing a baseball hat so his dark curly hair circled his head like a halo of question marks. Holy cow, those were pronounced cheekbones, steep as embankments. And that Sheriff of Nottingham goatee? I must've been an idiot to find that threatening. He wasn't the Sheriff of Nottingham. He wasn't even Robin Hood. Robin Hood was an outlaw. I'd had my fill of outlaws.

No, he was more than that. He was Good King Richard, home from the Crusades, ready to put everything right in the land.

And I cried then, because I'd come so close to missing this that I felt like I'd already missed it. That woke him up. He and asked me what was wrong, I didn't have any snappy answers. Then he surprised me. Instead of calling a nurse for more drugs, he gently lifted my head and put his arm around me. Without speaking, the two of us together drifted off.

∽

Gretchen and I are still standing under Portlandia when Tomás comes trotting up to us. Clean-shaven for the day. I run my fingers over his smooth jaw. I miss the scratchiness.

"Don't get used to it, babe," he says. "I'm growing it out as soon as the trial's over."

"Got the beeper?" I ask.

Tomás tosses it like a jump shot and catches it. "Your dad said to stick around," he says. "He doesn't expect them to deliberate long."

Gretchen points to a Starbucks across the street and I step-swing over. They are faster than I am. I try not to mind. With a little luck and physical therapy, I should be able to run again in the fall.

"That was smooth, your dad having you wear a miniskirt," Gretchen says as she scores a table for us outside on the red brick sidewalk. In front of us on the street, Tri-Met buses stop and start, peppering us with exhaust.

I look down at my leg, the one in the Frankenstein-like brace. There's a pin holding my tibia together. In two weeks the cast will come off and I'll get a boot. And even though Keith's dead, I'm still mad at him, shooting my leg so full of bone shards they found some wedged in my uterus. At least that's what Dr. Zegzula said. I think he was trying to make a joke.

Today, Dad insisted on the miniskirt so everyone can get a gander at what Phil LaMarr's dead stepson did to me. Dad kept saying something about the swing vote, and how jurists who might be interested in cutting Phil a break are less likely to after the parade of misery, Gretchen's testimony, my testimony, the Brads' testimony. The list of charges against Mr. LaMarr is long. He's an accessory to murder, but that seems to be the least of it. The big ones are masterminding a meth lab and owning unregistered firearms to protect it.

"Usual?" Tomás says, and goes in for caffeine: tall latte for him, mocha for me, Venti cappuccino for Gretch. I watch him progress through the line inside.

Out here, Gretchen lights a new cigarette from the butt of her old one. "Before I forget, I've got something for you," she says, reaching into her book bag. She draws out of pile of paper folded in half, and slides it across the table to me.

"What's this?"

"I was online the other day and I Googled *la llorona.*"

I groan, embarrassed I told her about that. I only mentioned it in passing in Group one Sunday at Riverside. I thought she'd get a kick out of it. You think you're the only freaky one? Get this: I was so delusional I thought the river was sending me messages.

I unfold the paper she's slid toward me and see a stack of printed-out articles. *Dark Beginnings of La Llorona. La Llorona Sighted by Border Guard. La Llorona And Elvis Have Demon Baby in Wal-Mart.*

"Thanks," I say unenthusiastically.

"She's a witch in almost every story. But in one of them she's a *curandera.* A healer. You know, helps lost children find their way out of the woods. That kind of thing."

She takes a drag on her cigarette, then stubs it out under her heel.

"It makes sense if you think about it. I mean, weren't the European witches really midwives? Then a bunch of men decided they had too much power? I think *la llorona* may have just gotten a bad rap."

I wonder if Gretchen is right. I try to remember: did *la llorona* ever try to lure me in? Or did she warn me, encourage me? *Run, Ronnie, run!* Maybe there's truth to what Gretch says. I don't know, but I'm glad she looked it up for me. The Gretchen from a year ago would've rolled her eyes and barked at me to let it go.

When Tomás comes back out he's smiling huge, carrying our drinks in a tray. "Up and at 'em. We're being beeped," he says. This is a good sign. They haven't even been deliberating half an hour.

We hobble back to the courthouse, under Portlandia, through the metal detectors, and up the elevator to our courtroom. Dad is sitting at the prosecutor's bench, waving at us as we all file in. On the bench behind him sits the Armstrong family. Mr. Armstrong squeezes over to make room for us. They do not look optimistic — not even the surviving kids. They know, as we all do, that this is not a happy day. But an undercurrent, deeper than optimism, has driven us here to witness it.

We are together for the first time since the day they

pulled me up onto dry land: Mom, Tiny, Ranger Dave, Gloria Inez, Mrs. Kinyon, the Brads, Gretchen, Tomás, and me.

I don't know what's going to happen to Phil LaMarr, but whatever it is, it won't be enough. Karen is gone, and those of us left are scarred, patched together with pins and braces and memories — all thanks to this man and his cottage industry that cost us so much.

I close my eyes, drowsy with heat and fatigue, and listen for something I know I won't hear. We're too far away.

But I don't really need the river. Because now I know the important stuff. I know that the Armstrongs might recover, encircling their remaining children like a mountain range, but they will never be the same. I know that Tomás and I are in love but we're living in separate cities, so staying together is impractical. I don't care, though, because when faced with something much stronger than us, we held on to each other and survived. I know how hard Gretchen is fighting for her future, but I also know that the statistics for people recovering from her particular brand of poison aren't good. If she wants to stay straight, she'll have to exert her will every day for the rest of her life. It is far from a perfect existence.

"All rise."

We stand for the judge to come in, then have to stay standing for the jury. It seems like a long wait, and I list like a tall tree in a high wind.

But at last the jury files past, and one of them darts a poisonous glance at Phil. Even before they deliver their verdict I know what they're going to say.

Mr. Armstrong reaches for my hand and squeezes it hard.

I listen for the Santiam but don't hear it.

This is the most important thing: those of us left standing are wobbly, but at least we're standing together.

It's enough, the river would whisper. *It's enough*.

ACKNOWLEDGMENTS

Once again I had the good fortune to have the backing of a great independent bookstore. A giant thank you to the Pages and co. at Island Books for moral support and letting me tinker on this project in the children's department.

Another big thanks goes to Lieutenants Autumn Fowler and Lisa Flores of the Bellevue Police Department for letting me ride along and opening my eyes about how bad the meth epidemic really is. ("Let's go! Shots have been fired! We need to move now!" "But . . . but . . . I brought lattes!")

Kit Close of Ranch Records in Salem, Oregon, graciously supplied me with the original Tiny story, which sparked my imagination but unfortunately didn't make it into the final novel. If you're ever in Salem, stop by the store and have him tell it to you. It's a good one.

Steven Chudney is a wonderful agent. I'm glad he's on my team. I'm also really fortunate in Jennifer Hunt and T.S. Ferguson at Little, Brown, who saw an earlier, amorphous version of the novel and took a chance on it even though it needed gutting. Thanks for a) staying with me and b) giving this project its shape.

Peggy King Anderson provided valuable feedback on more drafts than I can count.

My family, Juan, Sofia, and Ricky, gave me love, patience, and M&Ms. Did I hit the jackpot or what?

And finally, thank you to Gretchen and Kristin for being better friends than I deserved when I was growing up. I miss you both.

A Note From the Author

My editor and I first started discussing the paperback edition of *Dark River* at the same time Amy Winehouse died. It was July 2011, and you couldn't turn on a radio station without hearing Winehouse's gritty, soulful voice singing, "They tried to make me go to rehab but I said, 'No, no, no.'" Everyone I talked to at the time said (only half jokingly), "Why couldn't she have said, 'Yes, yes, yes'?" Such a talent, we all agreed. Such a waste. Couldn't someone have done something more to help her?

The question really bothered me, because I realized that, even though I've written a book about the devastating effects of addiction, I didn't have had any idea what to do in reality. I'm not a health care professional. My CPR certification is expired. I might be able to apply a Band-Aid or call 911. But what about in-between cases, like when someone you love is using and you want them to stop?

Time and again since the initial publication of *Dark River*, I've talked to schools and English classes and book groups and have been stupefied at how little I actually know. No matter how big an audience I've spoken to, and no matter where, there was always someone with hollow eyes sitting in the back who would come to me after the talk saying, "I think my friend is tweaking," or worse, "I think my father's dealing the stuff."

These were communities where I had no local ties, no idea where to refer them for resources. I could only stammer the words "guidance counselor."

I would watch as their eyes glazed over with disappointment. They wanted serious, concrete help, and my hands were so empty they might as well have held running water.

Thankfully, for the paperback edition of the book, I've been able to find plentiful resources to help you and the people you love deal with addiction. Dr. Robert C. Galak of The Evergreen Clinic of Kirkland, Washington, graciously pointed me to some online resources, listed at the end of this note.

According to The Partnership at Drugfree.org (www.drugfree.org), there are four steps that parents and loved ones can make to help addicts: *Prevent. Intervene. Get treatment. Recover.*

These are my thoughts on each step.

PREVENT:

Even though this part of the message seems to apply mostly to parents and guardians, there are all kinds of ways friends can help someone not develop an addiction at all. First, don't make anyone feel like a wuss for not indulging. Those of us who opt out have a variety of reasons. Some, like me, might be genuine wusses who are allergic to everything. Others might be smarter and know about dopamine, and know that part of the process for creating meth includes rat poison (yes, rat poison).

Also, if you get a "bad vibe" about any situation (especially at parties), *get out*. Most parents I know will gladly pick up their children wherever they are, especially if the alternative includes illegal substances. Illegal substances and cars? Yeah. Most of us will be there in a flash. Our nightmares aren't about our children in rehab; our nightmares are about our children dead at the side of the road or on someone's cold bathroom floor.

INTERVENE:

This can be a difficult one, but still important, because, especially with meth, casual use can quickly become dependency. One thing you might consider doing is suggesting your buddy "check himself" (www .checkyourself.com), to take a look in the mirror and figure out where they're at. No matter how you decide to intervene, be sure to *withhold judgment*. Addiction is a monster all of its own. An addict isn't more weak-willed than you are. Most drugs, especially meth, are engineered to create dependency. Blame the dealers. Blame the traffickers. Don't blame the friend who needs your help.

GET TREATMENT:

There are all kinds of residential facilities available. And while that's one option, there are plenty more out there. It's possible to detox without moving into lockdown. The Partnership at Drugfree.org website has an e-book titled *Treatment* (http://timetogethelp.drugfree.org/sites/default/ files/treatment_guide.pdf) that can give you more information.

RECOVER:

This is where a friend can really help. If a recovering addict relapses, understand that this happens and help your friend learn from their mistakes. Avoid judgment. Listen to their stories. Make sure they know that they are not alone.

I'm pleased to be able to include some resources in the paperback edition of *Dark River*. I want you all to know that, even though I can't be with you in person, you can think of me as *la llorona*—insubstantial as water, but still by your side, encouraging you on your long journey home.

Online resources, current as of the date this book was written:
- www.drugfree.org
- www.themethproject.org
- www.teens.drugabuse.gov
- www.checkyourself.com